MAID
FOR THE
TYCOON

LACEY LEGEND

This is a work of fiction. Similarities to real people, places or events are entirely coincidental.

Written by Lacey Legend

BOOK DESCRIPTION

To me, Billionaire Business Tycoon Spencer Lawson was beautiful. Perfect. My secret crush.

But to him, I was just "Jenna the Maid". The hired help who cleaned his Manhattan penthouse, did his laundry and cleaned up after all of the many women he had stay over.

In fact, I doubt he even knew my name since he actually never said a word to me.

But then one day everything changed...

As I cleaned his apartment, I caught him checking me out. He then caught me checking him out. And before I knew it, we were both indulging in flirty banter.

One thing soon led to another and from that point on, we both knew our relationship as we knew it was about to take on a whole new meaning...

Table Of Contents

Chapter One

Jenna swung open the door of the fifties-style diner. Her hazel eyes scanned the buzzing activity. It was full of hungry breakfast customers wolfing down pancakes, bacon and scrambled eggs. Spotting Kelly, Jenna tentatively waved her hand and hoped the expression on her face conveyed to her friend the desire for a quick chat. Kelly tapped the watch on her wrist and held up two fingers to Jenna, signaling she could have a break in two minutes.

Jenna waited by the breakfast counter and slipped onto the first red stool available. Her eyes followed Kelly around as she passed out overloaded plates to grumpy customers and refilled empty coffee mugs. Swinging the coffee jug over the counter for one of her co-workers to collect, Kelly rested her elbows on the cool steel of the bench and dropped her head back, taking a huge breath and closing her eyes as she exhaled.

"Tough morning," observed Jenna.

Kelly knew the question was rhetorical.

"They always are; doesn't matter which day of the week. Breakfast shifts are the pits."

"Yeah, I know."

"You did," corrected Kelly. "Since you've scored this exclusive cleaning job, your life has got a hell of a lot easier."

"You sound peeved."

"I am a bit," confessed Kelly.

The soles of Kelly's feet hurt. She knew however, no matter how much perfume and deodorant she doused herself in, the beads of sweat would continue running down her face for the duration of the shift. When she got home, she would reek of fried food and hard labor.

Jenna's heart-shaped face dropped and studied the floor. She wasn't too sure how to respond to her best friend's brutal honesty. She twirled a honey gold strand from her short frizzy hair between her fingers.

Kelly felt guilty begrudging her friend's good fortune.

"Don't mind me," said Kelly breezily. "I had a bit of a late night partying. It's my fault I'm feeling rough today. Nobody forced me to drink and I knew I had the opening shift. I could've called it an early night at a reasonable time if I'd had a responsible bone in my body."

"Still it's horrible feeling like that when you've got no support from the team."

The girls looked at the team of women who were considerably older than the two college girls, significantly overweight and wearing forced friendly expressions.

"Okay, I'm fuming because I've lost my work buddy. The only thing I resent is my laziness in not following your lead and using my initiative to get a decent job to get me out of this cesspool," confided Kelly. "What are you doing here anyway? You should be making the most of the weather," her voice lightened as the momentary resentment passed.

"No can do. I have a job to do myself today. Thought I'd grab a milkshake and have a quick chat before I go."

"What's he like?" asked Kelly.

"The billionaire?"

Kelly's blue eyes widened at the prospect of some seriously juicy gossip. "He's a billionaire?"

Jenna nodded, looking like the cat that got the cream.

"Is he hot?"

"He's buff and beautiful." giggled Jenna.

"Is he old?"

"Not like a granddad. He's," Jenna paused, " mature."

"A father-figure," teased Kelly.

Jenna pulled a face and wrinkled her nose. Kelly was fully aware Jenna had been raised by a single mother. The thought of her friends assuming she was looking for a father-figure to love was too ridiculously Psych 101 for words.

"No! He's in his late twenties or early thirties. From what I've seen of him on the phone, he's super charming, super intelligent, super witty and just plain...."

"Super."

"I sound silly, don't I?" asked Jenna, relieved her coffee colored skin hid her blushes.

"Super silly and super in love,va" cooed Kelly.

"Oh shut up. I've been working there for under a month."

"And he's a billionaire? You must be on a bomb. No wonder you aren't struggling for a wage."

"I am expected to work," Jenna defended exasperatedly. "And I'm not paid cash in hand by the boss. I'm employed by an agency, don't forget. They take a huge percentage of what he's actually charged. I'm left with little more than you are at the end of the week."

"If it's a boutique company that provides a maid or cleaning service to billionaires and that type of social class, I refuse to believe you're on minimum wage and reliant on tips to cover your weekly expenses."

"I came here for a girly chit chat, not to have my accounts scrutinized by someone who didn't even attain the grades to complete a business major."

Kelly laughed in good humor at the jibe. She knew she wasn't the brains of New York and Jenna was justified in delivering the cutting barb.

"Forgive me. I've put two and two together and got four billion."

Jenna couldn't help but guffaw at the ridiculous discussion. "Well I haven't got four billion," assured Jenna.

"You're just working for someone that has."

"Yes, I am," sighed Jenna.

"You actually do like him, don't you?"

Kelly could see from her friend's face the impromptu visit wasn't to boast about her hunky new client. She was smitten by the billionaire and looking for relationship advice.

"What's the plan?" probed Kelly.

"There is no plan. He's out of my league. He doesn't even notice me; at least I'm doing my job well."

"Because he tips big?"

"He doesn't tip at all. That would be considered gauche by these kinds of people. I mean the fact that I'm invisible, is supposed to be a good thing in this position. When I was interviewed to go on the books of Supreme Cleaning Services, Ms. Princely informed me to embrace the concept of being seen and not heard. I even had to sign an agreement whereby I'm not allowed to disclose or discuss anything I've seen or overheard in the premises that I work on." explained Jenna.

"It sounds very cloak and dagger."

"It's not interesting. I think it's more to do with respecting the privacy of the high profile clients. If there's questionable antics or undercover operations taking place, I haven't been exposed to them."

Jenna traced her finger in some spilt salt. Subconsciously she drew a heart.

"Kelly. You said two minutes. It's been closer to ten. Get your fanny back behind the counter and help to pick up the slack. Whatever dream boat you two girls are discussing can wait," yelled the short order cook.

"Can it wait?" inquired Kelly of her seemingly

confused friend.

"Sure it can. Of course, it was silly of me to corner you in a busy period." assured Jenna.

"What about your milkshake?"

"That'll have to wait as well. I need to start work soon and I can't afford to be late."

"Phone me later?" called Kelly. "I want the full details."

"I promise I will," retorted Jenna, as she squeezed through the crowd onto the street to make her way toward the Tribeca area of lower Manhattan.

*

Jenna preferred cleaning Spencer Lawson's penthouse apartment on a Saturday. It meant she never had to see him and thus couldn't become flustered and distracted in his presence. Given it was her duty to give the residence a full cleanup she really couldn't afford to spend half her time with one eye on his gorgeous looks and her mind creating a fantasy where the British billionaire would fall madly in love with her. Without Spencer in close proximity, she could get down and dirty to make the apartment spectacularly clean to the high standards her agency promised.

On weekdays before classes, Jenna was merely expected to ensure the bedroom was tidy, the bed made up, the kitchens, and bathrooms were immaculately cleaned and that she ran a vacuum cleaner around. Saturdays she had to clean every room from top to bottom and do the laundry.

Walking into the bathroom to grab the laundry basket, she caught sight of herself in the full-length mirror.

"No wonder Spencer barely acknowledges my existence," she thought as she examined her reflection.

The crisp white polo shirt with the agency emblem on the breast pocket, coupled with blue jeans and a blue apron were not particularly flattering to the figure.

"Practical – yes! Seductive – No!" thought Jenna. "Maybe the idea of these uniforms is to prevent us teasing the carnal urges of male clients. Although the idea of Spencer being so overcome by lust he takes me roughly in the kitchen isn't the worst scenario I can imagine. I'd happily trade this uniform in for a tacky French maid's outfit if it meant luring Spencer in the bedroom."

Jenna realized even with Spencer absent from the apartment, she was still fixated on him and wondered how she might catch his attention. Shaking her head, as if to rid the billionaire from her mind, Jenna lifted the dirty clothesbasket. She made her way to the laundry, hidden subtly behind sleek timber doors. As the majority of Spencer's suits were dry clean only, she was fortunate, as there wasn't an abundance of washing to do. Separating the colors from the whites, she began to load the washing machine.

Pausing before starting the cycle, she knew there was another room she needed to check for dirty laundry before she pressed the start button. With heavy feet, Jenna made her way to Spencer's bedroom. Her stomach felt knotted as she stepped in. She realized her eyes were closed.

Spencer Lawson's bedroom really was the most depressing scene, in Jenna's opinion. There was a reason her services were required six mornings a week. Spencer pretty much had a different partner every night; hence, fresh sheets were required daily. As one glamorous woman left the revolving door of the main reception of Spencer's high-rise building, a new one would be making her way in with an overnight bag to entertain the billionaire for an evening. Jenna wondered if the women were aware they had a twelve-hour expiration date in Spencer's life. Possibly they did.

Opening her eyes, she leaned against the doorframe of his bedroom. Weirdly, she wasn't jealous of the stream of wealthy, model-esque looking women he entertained. Sure, they might get to have sex with the dashing and debonair bachelor, but that was all. It appeared they meant very little to him emotionally.

"If I got Spencer, it wouldn't be for just a night," decided Jenna. "It'd be for life. What does it say about a woman who thinks of herself as nothing more than a one-night fling? No wonder he discards them like tissues."

She stripped the bed, hoping she wouldn't come across any women's lingerie caught up in the sheets that were twisted and disheveled from some seedy sex session. A smile spread across her face as the sheets appeared to have nothing more in them than a handkerchief embroidered with Spencer's initials.

As she started walking out of the room to take the sheets to the laundry, she heard something break underfoot of her practical black sneaker. Staring down at the floor, Jenna lifted her foot to see lipstick smeared on the bottom of her shoe and on the polished wooden floors.

Angrily she snatched up the plastic pieces of the lipstick tube and flung them in the nearby waste basket in the bedroom.

He had been with yet another woman last night.

"At least the floor's polished. I wouldn't want to be

on my hands and knees attempting to get that shade of violent red lipstick out of carpet."

Returning to the laundry, she set the machine in motion and retrieved her cleaning materials.

Debating on whether to start with the bathroom or kitchen, Jenna's least two favorite jobs, she opted for the en-suite bathroom. She plugged in the headphones of her iPod and set to work. Busying herself to the beats of her favorite playlist, Jenna was finally able to focus on the task on hand.

A hand on her waist made her yelp in shock and surprise. Spinning around and yanking the headphones from her ears, she was greeted by the vision of Spencer Lawson.

"Sorry to frighten you." he apologized in a warm baritone.

"No. I'm sorry."

"Sorry for what?" he asked directly.

The dark brown of his eyes was so intense Jenna was barely able to mutter a coherent sentence. He was right. She hadn't done anything wrong. Why did she feel the need to apologize? Spencer was staring at her, waiting for an answer. Jenna had been hoping the question was rhetorical.

"The headphones," she finally blurted out.

Spencer raised a quizzical eyebrow. Jenna's mind raced in a bid to justify her statement.

"It's only, I'm not sure I'm actually supposed to listen to music while I'm at work. If I hadn't had my headphones in I'd have heard you enter and made myself scarce."

"I certainly don't remember reading anything in the fine print of my contract with Supreme Cleaning Services stating that employees are forbidden from listening to music on personal devices," he said drily.

"No? Looks like I'm not on the firing line with Ms. Princely, then."

"Even if you were, I doubt it's a hanging offense."

"I suppose not."

They stood looking at one another in silence. *My first real conversation with Spencer Lawson and I come across as a ditzy moron,* thought Jenna.

"Anyway, my plans for the day have been altered and I've had to come home early. I'll do my best to keep out of your way." Spencer's voice was cool, but not unfriendly.

"I'm sorry to hear that," said Jenna automatically, in a

polite detached tone.

Spencer's chocolate eyes seemed to have a heat to them that was making her uncomfortable. They remained facing one another. Jenna wondered if she should just barge by him.

"What's your name?"

Jenna felt crushed. She'd been telling Kelly that Spencer barely recognized her existence on the planet, but deep down she'd been desperately hoping she'd made some kind of impression on him. That one question could only mean Spencer genuinely had no knowledge or interest in Jenna.

"It's Jenna. Jenna King."

"Jenna King, if you've finished in here and it appears you have, then I would very much appreciate the opportunity to use my en-suite. There's very little point in me sitting around the house all day in a three piece suit."

"Geez, sorry. Of course," blabbed Jenna.

The hint of a smile played on Spencer's kissable lips. The bottom lip was a touch thicker than his upper lip and when one side curved upward he looked positively dreamy.

Spencer took a step forward. Jenna failed to anticipate

which direction he was going to take and found herself colliding with him as she stepped out of the bathroom. Crashing against his six foot two frame, she felt pure muscle underneath the tailored suit. Spencer immediately had one hand on her waist and the other on her upper arm to steady Jenna. He might not be able to see her blushes, but Jenna knew he could feel the heat of her embarrassment emanating from the pores of her skin.

"I'll leave you to get on with things, Jenna King."

Completely flummoxed, Jenna wasn't sure where to start. At that precise moment, she was imagining a naked Spencer changing his clothes in the bathroom and that mental image had her hot and bothered. What did billionaires do with their days off when at home? Should she clean the bedroom in case he wanted to put his feet up? Was it best to start on the living room if he wanted to waste the day watching sports on TV? Perhaps he enjoyed cooking, in which case the kitchen would need to be done promptly.

This is a joke, thought Jenna, *sitting on a couch, how on earth do I get this man to notice me when I fall to pieces the first time we exchange words.*

"Right, I'm off to the gym."

Jenna looked up from the couch. Spencer was dressed in baggy knee length shorts and a tight sleeveless shirt. She could see how toned his legs were and the top stretched across his torso hinted at a flat stomach and pumped chest. Realizing she was staring in awe at Spencer from his couch, she jumped up from the sofa straight away.

"Sorry, I actually don't spend my time listening to music and resting on your couch when I'm supposed to be working."

Spencer laughed and the sound was musical to Jenna's ears. There was a richness and warmth to it. "As long as the apartment's clean, that's all I care about. If you do that by lying on my couch and casting a spell whereby the hoover and mop work without human interaction, that's fine by me."

"Sadly I'm at NYU, not wizardry school."

"I suspect both of those education institutions would have their benefits," grinned Spencer.

"Wizardry school might be more fun," said Jenna lightly, enjoying the idea of creating a love potion to slip to Spencer.

"Possibly. What are you studying at NYU?"

Oh my days, he's asked a question about me that isn't to do with work, Jenna thought excitedly.

"I'm completing a bachelor of science, specializing in

social work."

"That's...commendable."

Jenna felt a flicker of annoyance. Was he mocking her?

"I'm not looking for praise. I'm looking to contribute to society," she responded sharply.

Spencer saw she was stung by his comment. The silly schoolgirl air he'd detected earlier had been abandoned completely. The cleaner obviously took her studies seriously.

"I wasn't being flippant," he remarked. "I think any individual taking time out to study in the heady days of their late teens or early twenties and placing themselves in debt as a means of contributing positively to society is a commendable act."

Jenna wasn't sure what to say. It dawned on her that she'd come close to reprimanding her employer for a perceived judgment on her career choice. This was not remotely close to Ms. Princely's ethos of being seen and not heard.

"I should probably get on with cleaning," started Jenna in a composed manner. "The sooner I get this done, the sooner I'm out of your hair."

That lovely thick, curly brown hair I want to run my

fingers through, she thought, damn him for being so attractive I can't be angry by his patronizing air.

"It's no problem. Take your time. I'll be at the gym anyway."

*

The spacious apartment was borderline pristine. Jenna was taking her frustration regarding her earlier interaction with Spencer out on her cleaning. She scrubbed so hard; the place was sparkling. Had Spencer's ominous return been imminent, she would've sat on the black leather sofa and put her feet up to recover from her exhaustive bout of cleaning. Instead, she stomped to the laundry to replace every bottle of bleach, every tin of spray polish, every rag and every piece of cleaning equipment. Having taken out the final load of clothes from the dryer, she slammed the laundry door shut.

"You're very enthusiastic with your work, aren't you," came a familiar voice.

Now he is mocking me, grimaced Jenna.

"I aim to please and those laundry doors can get awful sticky sometimes."

"On rollers? Do I need someone to come in and oil them up so that they roll smoother? If it requires that much effort to close them, perhaps I should get a handyman in to take a look. I don't want you exerting yourself any more than you do with your thorough cleaning." He knew her temper got the better of her and was calling her bluff.

"Would you prefer it if I was lackadaisical and slap dash with my work?" she challenged.

"I'd prefer it if you didn't trash my apartment in the process," he countered.

"I'm just fed up," she snapped.

Spencer found the revelation both shocking and refreshing. He wasn't used to the hired help being brutally honest with him. His previous cleaner glided in and out of his apartment like a ghost. Frankly speaking, he enjoyed the arrangement.

Spencer wasn't the type to get too embroiled in anyone's life. This cute Afro-American girl had an undeniable sparkle that made him curious about her. He wasn't, however, going to encourage her emotional outburst by asking what made her fed up.

His quiet stillness irritated her.

"Don't you get fed up?" she asked, mystified that he could remain emotionally detached.

"No."

"Not ever?" she pressed.

"Not ever."

"Geez. How does that work?"

Spencer wasn't the type to discuss his personal life with the hired help, but manners dictated he couldn't ignore her question.

"Because I manage my life effectively. I'm organized and in control. I make sure no situation arises that can make me 'fed up'."

"You weren't fed up when your plans today were cancelled?" she enquired slyly.

"No. I'm always sure to consider any potential or unexpected changes in strategies. I have a contingency plan to fall back on if events result in me straying from my original plan."

"I'm not sure if that means you lead a very boring life or a very secure one."

"Let me assure you, Jenna King, my life is far from boring." replied Spencer curtly.

"Don't I know it!" commented Jenna in reference to his bedroom that seemed to operate like a busy airport terminal.

The tension mounted considerably after Jenna's

offhand remark. That kind of sass was a disciplinary offense. She had no right to discuss or assume anything about her client's lifestyle that she may have attained from cleaning the premises. Jenna was loathe to apologize, although she recognized she'd crossed a line.

She was proud of the fact that she worked to support herself and contribute to her family. There was no shame in cleaning, but she did object to anyone that considered her "lesser" because her employment was considered menial. She couldn't afford pride to stand in the way of keeping her job. She swallowed down her anger and did her best to look contrite.

"I'm sorry. It's none of my business."

"No, it's not." agreed Spencer, his voice icy.

His pompous attitude irked her.

"Just like it's none of your business what I'm studying at university."

"I don't suppose it is."

Spencer's tone was one of disinterest. He turned his back on Jenna and walked down the hallway to his bedroom.

Jenna was finished, but wasn't quite sure how to conclude her shift. Should she slip out quietly, locking the door behind her as was her usual practice? That custom seemed fine when she and Spencer never conversed. Having broken the ice with a prickly conversation, it appeared rude to leave without a verbal goodbye.

Bracing herself for another one of Spencer's dismissive interactions she made her way to his bedroom. Knocking lightly on the door she discovered he was no longer there.

I'm not in the mood for a game of hide and seek, she thought. She tiptoed toward the study where the door was half closed. Mustering her courage, her fist rapped hard on the doorframe.

"You're off?"

"Well you didn't invite me to stay for coffee," said Jenna.

She could sense a change in Spencer's posture. He'd relaxed. Slowly he twirled his seat around. Stretching out his long legs clad in beige chinos he smiled softly at her.

"It wouldn't be the done thing would it?"

Is he implying under other circumstances he would like to share a coffee, thought Jenna.

"I'm not sure. My mum spends a lot of time gassing

with the people she cleans for. Sometimes I think they look forward to her company more than her actually cleaning."

"Does your mum work for Supreme Cleaning Services, too?"

Jenna knew Spencer was highlighting the difference in class of her mother's customers and the high-class clients Supreme Cleaning Services catered to.

"No. She's an independent woman. Never had to rely on a company finding work for her. She was perfectly capable of getting off her own butt to find a job."

"You admire her?"

"Yes. And I adore her."

"Evidently," muttered Spencer.

Jenna guessed she'd shamed Spencer somewhat.

"I only came to tell you I'd finished and ask if there was anything further you needed doing."

He shook his head and his curly brown locks fell in his eyes.

"I'll be in on Monday morning and I'll be sure to keep my professional distance."

Spencer opened his mouth and shut it quickly.

Whatever goodbye he'd deigned to utter died on his lips. His brown eyes followed her out of the room and he listened carefully until he heard the front door lock. Shaking his head, he put his head in his hands. Jenna King was not the kind of girl for him to be targeting as a conquest.

Chapter Two

"Liana," called Jenna as she entered the small two-bedroom apartment her family shared in the Bronx.

"Shhhh. I've just put the baby down."

Jenna nodded at her younger sister, acknowledging the requirement to keep her voice low.

"How was work?" whispered Liana.

"It was work."

"Don't be weird. What kind of an answer is that?"

"The kind that tells you I don't want to talk about it."
.

"More racy thongs found in Mr. Billionaire's bed sheets?" teased Liana.

Jenna could never stay in a bad mood for long.

"No. But I did crush some poor random woman's lipstick and smear it all over the wooden floors."

"And this is a guy you have a crush on?"

"I'm not sure I do anymore."

"Why?"

Jenna shrugged her shoulders. She loved her sister to

death, but Liana had a habit of telling her mum every little secret Jenna disclosed to her.

"Sis, I've just got in from work. I'm not in the mood for the Spanish inquisition."

"I was only showing an interest in my big sister's life."

Jenna felt bad. Liana had somehow managed to get herself pregnant during freshman week. Liana had been the brains of the family and obtained a scholarship to Stanford University. Becoming pregnant meant she couldn't keep up with her studies and had to leave the prestigious university.

At just twenty, she now had an eighteen-month-old baby and attended night classes during the week when Jenna was able to take over babysitting duties. The father of little baby Zada had dropped off the face of the planet, leaving Jenna and Liana's mum taking on extra work to support the new addition to the family. Liana shared one bedroom with Zada and Jenna shared a bed with her mother in the other bedroom. It wasn't an ideal living situation, but the women were a tight-knit family and wouldn't be without Zada for the world.

"I know and I appreciate it. I'm in a mood today that's all. Ignore me. How's Zada been today?"

"Good as gold," beamed Liana proudly.

She may have missed her first opportunity to attend university, but Liana took to motherhood exceptionally well and for the most part, found it very rewarding.

"Mum's due back at six," announced Liana, changing the subject from the mystery billionaire seeing as it affronted her older sister so much. "You planning on going out tonight?"

With university, work and caring for her niece, Saturday was Jenna's only night off. The trouble was she was normally too shattered to make the most of her free night.

"I might ring Kelly. Check out what's going on."

Liana's face was green with envy. While her mother had supported her through thick and thin, she was never one to permit Liana to shirk her duties. After all, she'd been foolish enough to get pregnant and it was only fitting that she dealt with the consequences. Her break from baby Zada was attending night classes because they had an educative purpose. Nights out for drinking and dancing were not a luxury a new mother could afford. Liana understood this, but being only twenty, she was often wished for the lifestyles her friends were living.

"Do you want to go out tonight?" asked Jenna.

"Seriously?"

"Seriously. My treat. I'm too tired to go out, if I'm being honest. I can stay in and babysit Zada and prepare dinner for mom and you can pop out and remember what it's like to be young, free and single again."

Liana's squeal of joy, as she flung her arMs. round her sister's neck, woke Zada. Jenna didn't mind. It was worth it to witness the look of appreciation and joy on her sister's pretty face. They sat in excited silence until Zada settled.

"You are the best sister in the world!"

"I know," grinned Jenna, "and I'm not even going to say you owe me one."

Liana was in her bedroom and on the phone within minutes of accepting Jenna's kind gesture. A little after 6 pm, the front door opened and Jenna's mother walked through. She looked exhausted, but was eager to check on her granddaughter as soon as she entered. Jenna went close to the cot to give her mother a quick kiss on the cheek.

"Your sister called me to tell me about tonight's arrangements. You're too soft on that girl. She's not the baby of the family anymore."

Jenna knew from the tone of her mother's voice she was only pretending to be cross.

"She'll always be my baby sister. However many nieces and nephews she pops out for me to be Aunty to, I'll always have my eye on her to make sure she's safe and happy."

"God forbid," said her mother. "Let's give her time to get an education and find a nice man so she does it properly next time around."

Jenna was going to remind her mother that their father had left them high and dry, but thought better of it.

"Thoughts for dinner?"

"I'd love a takeout," replied her mother, flopping on the sofa and putting her feet up. "But we can't afford it."

Jenna had already promised some of her pay to Liana. If she treated her mother to a takeout as well, she'd have a lean week until the following payday. What the hell, thought Jenna, how many sacrifices has she made for me over the years?

"I've got enough saved for a little treat tonight," lied Jenna. "As Liana's out, why don't we have a girly night and order in Chinese and watch trashy romantic films?"

Jenna's mother's eyes filled with tears. Her eldest daughter may have made a few poor errors of judgment in the past, but she had the kindest most generous heart of anyone she knew.

"Keep your money, sweetie. We'll rustle something up."

"No can do. You're too tired to cook and I can't be bothered. Once Zada's bathed and in bed you and I are going to hit the comfort food and entertainment," insisted Jenna.

"I'm too tired to put up a fight. Thank you very much, baby girl."

Keen for a break, Jenna went to her shared bedroom and dialed Kelly.

"How's my favorite exclusive supreme cleaner?" greeted Kelly.

"Terrible."

"Why?"

"Because the flat wasn't empty when I cleaned it today," moaned Jenna.

"Don't tell me one of his harlots was lounging in her lingerie."

"No. Worse than that – he was!"

"I'd have thought you'd have enjoyed the eye candy."

"I did. It was when he opened his mouth that it all went wrong."

"Have you never spoken before?" quizzed Kelly incredulously.

"No. I've always adored quietly in close proximity as he conducted his busy life. I never see him on Saturdays and usually on weekday mornings, he's leaving the apartment not long after I enter."

"Don't you say hi and bye?"

"No. It's minimal eye contact and a nod of the head," described Jenna.

"Well, that just sounds rude."

"What came out of his mouth was a lot ruder."

"Why? What did he say?"

Jenna thought this over.

"It can't have been that rude if you can't tell me immediately," pressed Kelly.

"It wasn't so much what he said but how he said it."

"Details, please!"

"For a start he had to ask me my name."

"That's no surprise. You said he didn't know you existed."

"Yes I said that," agreed Jenna, "but I didn't believe it. I'd hoped I may have caught his eye. If only by the high standard of my cleaning."

"He didn't know your name. That doesn't make him the big bad wolf."

"It seemed like he was mocking everything I said. From my studies to my presence in his house."

"Oh. That's not cool."

"No. It's dented my ego,big time."

"I can't imagine you just standing there and not saying anything back to him. Is he so good looking you turn mute when you're within a 5 mile radius of him?

Actually, he is that good looking. He's all brown curly hair, brown eyes, a strong jaw with stubble and he's built like a football player. Honestly, I'm not exaggerating when I say he looks like a Greek God."

"I'd love to see a pic."

"Forget your hormones for a second, Kel. I did stand up for myself."

"Good for you."

"No. I've potentially risked losing my job and I clearly annoyed him. I think it was better when he didn't know who I was. I suspect he now thinks of me as some kind of skin irritation, blotting his day when I enter his apartment."

"Perhaps you misread his body language."

"He turned his back and walked out on me mid-conversation."

It was Kelly's turn to be quiet.

"Jen, he doesn't sound like such a great guy. Can't you ask for a new client?"

"I don't want to look like I'm causing trouble. That old cow Ms. Princely will do some investigating if I put in a request for a change of client. I don't want to lose out on the job completely. Besides, for all I know, Spencer Lawson may already have terminated my contract with him."

"Spencer Lawson?"

"Yes."

"You realize he literally is worth billions?"

"Inherited no doubt," guessed Jenna cattily.

"No. He made his own fortune. He's in computers. Something to do with information technology and cloud computing."

"I wouldn't know," admitted Jenna glumly. "We can't afford an internet connection so the only time I use the internet is at NYU for coursework. I never thought to run a search on who he was."

*

Jenna was plodding unhurriedly from the subway to work early Monday morning. It was only a two-hour shift, but she was dreading it. Normally, she'd be full of vim and vigor, rushing to and from the subway, making sure she was on time for her first class at 10 on a Monday morning after her cleaning job. Despite the warm sunshine, Jenna wanted to stay curled up in bed to avoid Spencer Lawson and the university.

Spending quality time with her mother on Saturday night was splendid and discussing her sister's antics on Sunday was equally enjoyable, but today she was back to the real world. On the plus side, she hadn't received a call from Ms. Princely, so it appeared Spencer hadn't told tales of her brazen back-talk at work on Saturday. For that reason, she felt a degree of warmth toward the chilly billionaire.

Waving with an absence of enthusiasm to the doorman of Spencer Lawson's building, she slumped through the revolving doors at the same time a willow blonde was exiting.

Wonder if she lives here or if she was keep Spencer company last night, thought Jenna.

A petite five foot four, Jenna felt substandard when comparing herself to the mystery lady. With a backpack slung over her shoulder with clothes to change into upon arriving on campus, she felt frumpy in her uniform. There wasn't a crease in her apron or polo shirt. Signing in and attempting to exchange conversational pleasantries with the man at reception, Jenna made her way to the elevator.

Taking the keys from her handbag, she inserted a small one into a slot on the panel of buttons in the elevator. . Turning it clockwise, she was permitted to press the button to take her to the top floor to Spencer's penthouse suite. She forced herself to control her breathing. There was nothing to be fearful about. Spencer hadn't complained. All she had to do was continue as normal and fade into the background.

The mental pep talk she'd given herself, didn't improve Jenna's frame of mind. She slipped the keys in the door and used the fob to sneak into the apartment. The sound of her exhalation was audible upon discovering Spencer wasn't in the kitchen or living room. She bolted to the minimalistic white modern kitchen and attacked the dirty dishes.

Why on Earth can't he use a dishwasher, she mulled while scrubbing. *I understand that he built his own fortune, but that shouldn't preclude him from everyday tasks.*

As she conducted a private assassination of what little she knew about Spencer Lawson, the handsome English gent strode into the kitchen. Their schedules were out of sync that morning. Normally, she'd be finished with the kitchen by the time he was ready for breakfast and she'd be tidying his bedroom while he ate. A domestic, responsible part of her (the part that respected her position at Supreme Cleaning Services) was inclined to ask him if she could fix him something to eat. The part of her that thought he had an inflated ego from earning too much too young, decided he could fix his own breakfast.

As Spencer moved behind her, she experienced a frisson as his hard body brushed against her. She steeled her resolve to prevent her going weak at the knees. He felt solid and strong and she wanted to melt into him. Remembering that some other woman was melded with his body only hours earlier had her straightening her back and swiftly skipping out of his way. She watched as he put two crumpets in the toaster. Slowing her pace to that of a snail's, she studied him as he retrieved butter from the fridge and lathered it on the toasted crumpets.

God knows how he keeps trim eating fatty foods like that, she thought.

Leaving the butter on the counter and the toaster plugged in, he tossed the knife and plate into the dishwater. The water barely rippled enough to splash Jenna's apron, but she kissed her teeth at the action to demonstrate her disapproval.

A slow smile spread on Spencer's face. If Jenna didn't know better, she'd think he was trying to evoke a reaction from her. She held her head high and maintained her composure.

Spencer waited to see if the feisty girl would take the bait. He refused to let his disappointment show that she couldn't be drawn into talking to him.

Checking his watch, he decided to toy with Jenna a little longer. He sat at the marble breakfast bench and began reading the newspaper. The large spread of the paper covered a sizeable portion of the bench preventing Jenna from wiping it clean. With an exaggerated sigh, she drained the sink and wiped the dishes.

Rather than ask Spencer to move the newspaper, she decided to start on the bedroom and return to the kitchen after his departure. Spencer was a businessman. She knew from his habits he was an early starter at work. Whatever game he was playing this morning he'd soon tire of and head out to his offices.

Spencer bit the side of his cheek as Jenna left the kitchen. He was usually a good judge of character. It may have been a brief encounter, but he'd got the impression on Saturday that Jenna was a motivated, confident, high achiever. He admired those qualities and liked her spirit.

Talking with her had been unexpectedly fun. She challenged him and that was a rare quality in the women he mingled with. That she was a university student with a part time cleaning job and wasn't intimidated by him, made her all the more attractive in his eyes. Today though, she'd reverted back to being a faceless cleaner with no personal connection to him.

She was efficient, punctual and good at her job. It appeared as though that was all that was on offer to him. She'd intimated that his life was boring, but her ability to embrace a hands-off approach so readily after Saturday's encounter suggested her life wasn't overly stimulating. Clearly maintaining a professional facade was more important to her than engaging in a little flirty banter as they passed in and out of one another's lives.

Grabbing his briefcase and double-checking his pockets for his cell phone, keys and wallet, he discarded the potential plans he'd created for Jenna. He stuck his head round the door to see her making the bed up with fresh sheets and a distasteful look painted on her face.

The jeans, polo shirt and apron did nothing for her figure. He'd been attracted to her personality, but seeing her as a cleaner in his apartment, he realized he hadn't lost anything by not distracting Jenna. She was no major loss to him.

However, as he strode out of the apartment, he experienced a niggle inside that prevented him from focusing on the day ahead. It was irrelevant. Even with his billions, he couldn't buy Jenna's affections. He couldn't pay her to like him. Perturbed, he nodded at the receptionist and doorman and hopped in the limousine that routinely took him to work.

Jenna finished her tasks after a quick tidying of the apartment. She'd got through the shift without any awkwardness. Now Spencer was witness to the fact that she could behave as nothing more than a faceless, emotionless maid. That is what he'd wanted and that's what she delivered.

Jenna was relieved the following day to find Spencer's schedule was back in sync and their paths didn't cross until he left the apartment each morning with his normal brief nod.

Looks like work can revert to normal, she declared, somewhat disheartened, to the empty apartment.

Chapter Three

"Mr. Lawson's away for the next two weeks," stated Ms. Princely.

Jenna felt the view of Central Park from the 25th floor in a grand, but dim and darkened office of Victorian design, was a little extravagant for a cleaning agency – whatever the company's net worth was. The furniture was authentic and so aged, Jenna feared she might inadvertently break something when she was obligated to meet Ms. Princely from time to time in her employer's private office.

"He has, however, asked for you to continue tending to his apartment in his absence."

"As in I should visit the day before he's due back to clean the apartment thoroughly?" clarified Jenna.

"As is your current terms. Two hours in the morning on weekdays and half a day on Saturdays. This way it won't impact on your earnings for the two-week period."

Jenna was at a loss for words. There was very little for her to clean if no one was living in the apartment, but at the same time, she desperately needed a steady income stream.

Ms. Princely read Jenna's face accurately. Privately,

she too thought it was unnecessary for Jenna King to spend time in the apartment, but her job was to provide a service to Mr. Lawson, not question his decisions.

"You can at least keep it dust-free and I believe he'd like you to collect his mail and dispose of the newspapers. Make sure nothing is out of date in his fridge or cupboards."

The two women eyed each other, neither daring to intimate the comment that it was an odd arrangement. Ms. Princely was plump and barely reached five foot, but she was well dressed and had an air of a headmistress about her. Jenna didn't dare argue. Her conscious was pricked. Spencer may be able to afford her services, but he shouldn't throw his money away carelessly.

"Maybe I should cut my hours so that he's not paying me to sit around and...."

Ms. Princely smiled kindly at Jenna. The young lady was hard working and good hearted.

Clearly, Mr. Lawson saw those same qualities and didn't want to deprive Jenna of her regular income.

"Mr. Lawson trusts you. I suspect in terms. of security, he'd feel confident if someone he knew was checking in on the apartment daily. There may not be a lot for you to do in terms. of cleaning, but he's probably paying for peace of mind while he's abroad."

"His apartment building is like Fort Knox and I doubt his neighbors are petty thieves."

"Jenna. Stop talking yourself out of a job. Accept it with good grace. Maybe it is just a goodwill gesture, but is that the worst thing in the world?"

"No," Jenna answered quietly. I just don't want to think of arrogant Spencer Lawson being in possession of a beating heart, she thought.

***

The two weeks flew by. Although Jenna knew she only had to pop into the apartment for quarter of an hour a day, she always stayed for the duration of her shift; trying to find things to busy herself with.

Polishing the wooden floors one Friday morning, she heard the door open.

Spencer stepped in, dropping a suitcase. He was dressed casually in blue jeans and a white t-shirt. Apart from the time Jenna had seen him attending the gym, she hadn't ever seen Spencer dressed casually. Rather than ignore her, he smiled at her.

"Hi Jenna."

Jenna was stunned by his friendliness.

"Hi, Mr. Lawson." She wanted to ask if it was a good trip, but would that be considered an invasion of his personal life? "I do hope things went well for you while you were away," she said formally.

"As good as can be expected, thanks."

Jenna knew her mouth was smiling and she was flashing her pearly whites. It wasn't that he looked as if he'd stepped off a catwalk in Milan that made her happy, but the naturalness of the brief hello.

"Bedroom free for me to unpack?"

She nodded.

"Absolutely. Let me know if you need a hand with anything."

He ran a large hand through his locks. As his chiseled face was cleared from the curls she could see his face was pale and his eyes had bags under them. Jenna suspected he was jetlagged.

"I can scoot off, if you prefer to be by yourself," she offered.

"It's fine. Stay. I might need a hand in the bedroom," he laughed.

He's flirting with me, she thought, Or maybe he just

wants me to unpack his luggage. She remained in the living room polishing the timber floor over and over. Straining her ears, she could hear Spencer on the phone.

"Please tell me that text you sent earlier was a joke, because that is not the news I want to receive when I've just jumped off a five hour flight." There was silence as the person on the other end of the phone spoke. "I'm glad the publicity of a movie premiere is considered more valuable to her than attending a charity event."

"Someone famous has stood Spencer Lawson up," guessed Jenna.

"It's very late in the day for me to be finding another date and as this is a high profile function, what I need is a high profile date. Are you seriously telling me you have no one else on your books free and willing to attend tonight?" A long silence stretched. "I sponsored this event. My being absent isn't feasible. You promised me assistance with the guest list and now you're failing to deliver. If you can't come up with something, you can consider our professional relationship over."

"I do believe Mr. Lawson doesn't have a contingency plan for tonight," giggled Jenna, realizing Spencer was about to experience firsthand what it was to be 'fed up'.

"No," she heard him sneer. "I have no intention of hiring an escort for the night and I don't care which firms you'd recommend; it's tacky and unnecessary."

His final sentence appeared to terminate the call. Jenna could hear his boots stomping around the bedroom. She fled to put the mop in the laundry room and make herself scarce.

"Jenna," he called. His tone was firm.

"Mr. Lawson," she piped up from the laundry.

"Can I see you for a minute please?"

She made her way to the living room with an expression of naiveté and curiosity.

"Something I can help you with?"

"Perhaps, but it doesn't fall under the category of cleaning," he said slowly.

Her hazel eyes studied him and she realized he was scrutinizing her appearance and attempting to assess her character. She could see the brown eyes almost twinkling as the cogs in his brain were formulating some kind of plan.

"Why don't you sit down?"

Jenna accepted the invite. She resisted the urge to be humorous by kicking off her sneakers and half lying on the couch. Spencer didn't seem to be in the mood to find her faux insolence amusing.

"I'm in something of a bind," he started honestly.

Don't I know it, she thought.

"There's a rather major charity event on tonight for which I'm something of an ambassador for."

"That's...commendable," teased Jenna gently, throwing his own words back in his face.

"Touché," he conceded. "I need a date to accompany me. The lady I was paired with can't make it."

"Surely that little black book of yours is full of names of women that'd be more than happy to go with you."

Spencer took the barb in good humor.

"It's not a little black book," he corrected. "It's a big black book that's coming apart at the seaMs. with all the names and numbers I have in it."

Jenna laughed and shook her head at his arrogance.

"Besides," he continued. "They aren't appropriate for this event. I wondered if you might step in."

I do believe there was a compliment somewhere in there, thought Jenna, is he saying of all the wealthy, beautiful women he's bedded, little old me, a twenty-one year old student in her final year at NYU is more suitable for this highly important function? He's been stood up by some famous socialite or actress or singer and he thinks I'm the next best thing. Maybe he did notice me and I read him all wrong.

"What do you think? I'll make it worth your while."

"In what way?"

"Well I'll pay you for your time, of course. I was thinking $1000 for the evening. I'd hope that covers the cancellation of any other plans you've made."

He knows I couldn't afford to turn a sum like that down, grimaced Jenna inwardly, and, it'd make a huge difference to the family income. She felt hurt, but couldn't pinpoint why.

"Obviously I'll pay for transport to Macy's and you can buy whatever outfit you need and I'll have it put on my account."

Jenna suddenly realized why she was hurt, because this was nothing more than a business transaction to Spencer. Even though she was fully aware how important business was to him, and even though she knew how little women meant to him, she still wanted to be special to Spencer Lawson. Her enthusiasm waned. Pride would have her decline the invitation, but love of her family and the thought of extra savings for Liana and baby Zada would make her accept the offer.

"Sure. That sounds fine to me."

*

"Yes, I'm on my way," promised Kelly, on the phone to Jenna. "I'll be in ladies wear before you arrive."

"Well I'm in a cab now and I want the works done there. Not just the outfit, but hair and makeup too ," panicked Jenna.

"This is possibly the most exciting thing to happen in your life, next to your ex being jailed."

"Kelly!"

"Sorry. Too soon?"

"Too soon and seeing my boyfriend jailed wasn't exciting. It practically broke me and tore me apart from my family."

"Sorry, Jen."

Kelly's apology was more sincere. In all the thrilling news of Jenna's new appointment as British billionaire Spencer Lawson's guest for the evening, Kelly had been completely insensitive to her friend's past.

"It's okay. It's just... I don't like to think about it."

"I'll say no more about it."

"Kelly, I know you stood by me through that. Even though this is a professional engagement, you're right – I am moving forward in a good way."

"Jenna?"

"Yes."

"I'm in Macy's now and the selection and prices here are incredible. You can't afford to stint tonight by showing up in something shoddy."

"I know that's the best part. I can spend his money and not feel guilty," agreed Jenna as she paid the cab driver.

As Jenna swept in and gave Kelly a hug, the two girls squeezed hands.

"Good day, ladies," greeted a well-dressed woman. "Mr. Lawson has requested my services as a personal shopper should you require any assistance today. Now would you be Jenna?" she enquired shaking Kelly's hand.

"No," replied Kelly coolly. "This foxy lady is."

The personal assistant raised an eyebrow.

"You think Spencer Lawson doesn't do interracial dating," whispered Kelly to her friend. "Why target the blonde haired, blue eyed, ex cheerleader who never quite made it to college? Unless that's his normal type."

"Don't put yourself down," hissed Jenna. "Maybe she's got some sort of issue with the black and white thing."

"Well, I hate her," said Kelly.

"Kel, you're being overly loyal and defensive. It may be a genuine mistake. Thinking you were Spencer's date doesn't make her a racist."

"She might be. It'd be fitting to the plot."

"What? What on earth are you rabbitting on about?"

"Don't you feel like we're in a scene from a romantic comedy? You know a rags to riches affair?"

"Kelly, it's just one night and it's a job. Let's not get ahead of ourselves here."

"Hate them all," screeched Kelly petulantly as the personal shopper arrived with her first three selections of dresses.

The afternoon was fun. The personal shopper was efficient, effective and had an amazing eye for fashion and what suited Jenna's petite figure. Once the outfit was selected, the girls headed to the salon. Jenna opted to have her hair colored and straightened.

The honey gold afro was transformed into a sleek straight dark brown bob with warm red shades throughout. Her makeup was subtle and complimented the color of her dress. When the session was over and it was time for Jenna to return, the girls were disappointed they had to part.

"This will probably be the best part of the whole event," moaned Jenna.

Kelly assessed her friend. In her eyes, Jenna was always beautiful, but tonight she was stunning. As much as she loved hanging with Jenna and enjoying a taste of how the other half lived, Kelly wanted her friend to have a brilliant evening.

"No," said Kelly softly. "This is a great start to what is going to be one of the most memorable nights of your life. Take it for what it is, but don't miss a minute of it and don't for one second think you don't belong there. Spencer Lawson won't know what's hit him and if he can't see the girl of his dreams on his arm when he enters that posh charity do with you tonight, then he's blind and not worthy of your heart, anyway."

"Kelly, you're the best."

"And you deserve the best. I won't kiss you goodbye because I don't want to ruin your make up, but I'm overwhelmed by what I'm seeing. Get out of here before I get weepy."

"Join me in the cab. It can take you home after it drops me off," insisted Jenna.

"Back to Brooklyn from Manhattan? Won't Spencer question the fare?"

"It's my treat."

"Save your money Jenna. I'm happy to use public transport."

Jenna hopped in the cab her friend has flagged and felt a wave of sadness wash over her. She made a silent wish that Kelly would one day get a night like this so she too could feel like a princess for an evening.

Confidence in her appearance had Jenna striding through the revolving doors of Spencer's plush residence. However, confidence alone didn't permit her to pass the authoritarian uniformed man on reception.

"May I help you miss," he asked politely as he cut Jenna off from the elevator.

"Jenna King for Mr. Lawson."

"Miss King, I didn't even recognize you," he exclaimed. "You look a treat tonight. Forgive me; I'm not used to seeing you out of uniform."

"Think I'll do?"

"Whatever the occasion, I'm certain you'll make the right impression."

"Thanks," she winked as he indicated she enter the elevator.

Despite the approving glances and admiring comments on her way back to Spencer's, she suddenly felt nervous about his reaction. Everyone in this building was used to seeing her in jeans, a shirt and an apron. Turning up in her gym gear probably wouldn't have attracted as much attention.

She let herself into the apartment.

"Did you get on okay?" he shouted from the bedroom.

This has all got very informal very quickly, thought Jenna. "I think so," she replied, hoping she wasn't screeching.

"What do you mean think?"

Spencer stepped into the doorway frame of the bedroom leading to the living room. He was dressed in full white tie regalia, including a white bow tie, white waistcoat and stiff white dress shirt with a pique collar, coupled with black pleated trousers, black tails, and patent black leather oxfords. Spencer looked as though he'd stepped out of a scene from Downton Abbey. Before Jenna was able to compliment his attire, Spencer's eyes widened at the sight of her and his mouth dropped.

"You look amazing," he whispered huskily.

The six-inch gold heels emphasized Jenna's toned, slender legs under the olive-green and gold full length gown which was slit high to her thigh to show a flash of skin as she walked. There was no need for a plunging neckline to draw attention of her cleavage. The shoestring straps of the dress held the fitted bodice close to her firm rounded breasts and the soft material clung to her flat stomach.

"You look like a star."

"I feel like a star," said Jenna graciously. "Perhaps it's just the hint of gold sparkle from the dress," she laughed disarmingly.

"No," protested Spencer sincerely. "You do look unearthly. Not of this planet. Some beauty from far away to visit for the night."

"You sound almost poetic."

"That'd be the effect of your outfit," he grinned. "Imagine what I'll be like after a few glasses of champagne."

The atmosphere had changed in the room. Suddenly it didn't feel like a business arrangement anymore. Suddenly Jenna was looking forward to the evening and not because there was a $1000 check waiting at the end of it.

The telephone rang, breaking the surreal romantic air of Spencer's flat. His hand flew to it and he asserted that he'd be along promptly.

"Are you right to leave or do you need more time?"

"I'm good to go."

"You certainly are," affirmed Spencer, placing his hand on her back as he ushered her out the door.

*

"Anything you need to brief me on before we arrive?"

Spencer smiled at her. "Don't worry. It's going to be fine and you're going to be fine. Just be yourself and stick close to me."

Jenna felt reassured. Given Spencer was heavily involved with the charity she assumed he'd be expected to mingle and network for the majority of the evening, leaving Jenna to her own devices with a bunch of people she didn't know and wouldn't be able to relate to.

Seeing a bottle of champagne in an ice bucket as she entered the limousine, was a relief to Jenna's eyes. Spencer opening it and pouring them both a glass was equally as welcome. The bubbles of the expensive Moet were going to her head and calming her nerves for the night ahead.

"I hope I don't embarrass you."

"If I thought for a second you might, I wouldn't have invited you."

"Sometimes you sound like a real snob, but other times I think you're just a brutally honest kind of man."

"I'm not sure I'm the kind of man that can be bothered with tip toeing round people to spare their feelings. You get much more accomplished with people if you're up front and open with them. Playing games gets you nowhere. I don't have time to waste in my life," reflected Spencer.

"I'd have thought one of the bonuses to being a billionaire was that you could afford to waste time and play games."

"I can afford to do that, but I don't want to. You can't

buy time and some people unfortunately don't have the time, no matter how much money is thrown at them."

Jenna studied her hands and attempted to decipher Spencer's cryptic words.

"What charity is this event for tonight," she inquired.

"Rett syndrome."

Jenna hadn't heard of it. "Forgive my ignorance, but I'm not familiar with it."

"There's nothing to forgive. The majority of people haven't heard of it. That's why I'm hosting the event – to promote awareness. Now you've heard of it, I know I've accomplished something tonight."

"What is it?"

"It's a nervous system disorder. It's diagnosed in children as early as six months. Breathing problems, seizures, muscular problems. They have difficulty with using their hands and expressing themselves in terms of language."

"There's no cure is there," pre-empted Jenna.

"No," said Spencer, his puppy dog eyes were incredibly sad. "I keep hoping if we have the funds to invest, one day we might have a breakthrough. As it currently stands, if you're diagnosed with Rett Syndrome, you have a life expectancy of mid-twenties. Some live longer. If you are afflicted though, you don't have the luxury of playing games and wasting time."

"Who do you know who has it?"

"What makes you think I'm not the philanthropist type and this is just a hobby?"

"Because you look and sound like a human when you talk about it, rather than the arrogant, playboy image you like to project in my company."

"I'm British. I don't discuss my feelings," he said firmly, but softly.

"I'm from Brooklyn. I'm nosy and if I'm determined, I normally get the answers I'm after."

"I'd rather enjoy tonight. Let's drop it."

"That wasn't specified in my contract," pushed Jenna gently. "You've thrown this gala to raise money for a charity to help a person that's special to you. Don't insult my intelligence by implying you aren't going to give them a second thought the minute that we're out of this vehicle."

The limousine began to slow as it approached the club.

"My niece. I've been over visiting her in London. She's five. The countdown has already begun for that little girl. Now let's get to work."

As the chauffeur opened the door and offered a hand to Jenna to assist her out of the limousine she was stunned by the array of photographers snapping her. This clearly wasn't a low-key affair. Jenna didn't have time to feel out of her depths. Spencer had already laced his fingers through hers and pulled her protectively close to him. He deliberately took his time walking the red carpet to allow the avid paparazzi to photograph him and Jenna.

"What's it feel like to be on the arm of one of New York's most eligible bachelors?" he murmured in her.

"I can think of a thousand reasons why I'm enjoying it," she said sharply with a smile spread wide across her face.

"Ouch!"

"You were asking for that, big head."

"I suppose I was. But I feel more like five foot two now rather than my usual six foot two."

"Let me soothe your ego, you're one of the tallest, most beautiful bachelors in attendance."

"My real reasons for attending gives me the moral

high ground anyway."

"I thought you found schoolboy behavior and games wholly tedious."

"I do. But I feel myself dragged into an event that I can't cross my arms and walk away from, then I have to resort to such lowbrow tactics."

"Well, you could, if I had a modicum of commonsense."

"Jenna, look at me," he demanded, circling slowly to show off his honed physique in the tailored flawless materials of his suit that emphasized his masculinity. "The majority of cameras back there are for me – for us! It's imperative we stand out and make an impression."

"How so?"

"Because we're the ambassadors for tonight, We're the face of Rett Syndrome and to take that mantel, we have to out class, out talk and out beautify every other person on the guest list."

"That's an awful lot of work for $1000!" She murmured with a sly wink.

"You got your outfit for free, " he whispered in her shoulder letting his mouth down to nibble the bare chocolate of her flesh. Even before Jenna acknowledged them, Spencer could taste the gooseflesh raise on Jenna's skin from the softest brush of his mouth. Shivering, she shrugged her shoulders indicating Spencer should remain upright.

Jenna took a few steps ahead and found a board with the table seating displayed and where people were assigned their relevant seats and table numbers.

"We're together," she clasped her hands quietly. Thrilled to not have to be flung into the wilderness with rich bodies that she shared nothing in common with interest with. "Are we at the head table?"

"Uh-huh", replied a half-listening Spencer.

"Will there be toasts?"

"Yeah, yeah. There's a running order and master of ceremonies. Just chat and smile and look madly in love with me."

"Perhaps I'll settle with completely beguiled by you."

"That would work as well," agreed Spencer taking two glasses of champagne for him and Jenna.

She was surprised at the throng of people keen to network with Spencer. The dates of the men whom were cornering Spencer, were ogling the billionaire or sizing up his date – Jenna. She resisted the urge to bare her teeth and hiss like an alley cat. It would've made an impression, but probably not the impression Spencer wanted to make. . As they ambled around the pure white décor with dark plum drapes from the ceiling, Jenna was relieved to finally hear the bell ring for dinner.

She felt as though she were the bride of the wedding or in the prom seats at the head table.

"Are you going to make a toast soon and wish us long life and happiness," said Jenna, with a perfect smile, not divulging her wicked thought.

"Some other time, perhaps."

That Spencer was laughing at her cheek had Jenna flustered.. He may have been fooling but momentarily it made her feel that it wasn't out of the realm of possibilities.

Giving the enormous function room one final scan, the Maître d'hôtel tapped Spencer respectfully on the shoulder before slinking back into the shadows to the sidelines. Taking a deep breath, Spencer rose from his chair, picked up a fork and tapped itt on a glass so the sharply it clanged around through the hall.

"Let me start by thanking each and every one of you for attending. The money raised tonight isn't just to promote Rett Syndrome to raise awareness for every person on the street. Our aim is to continue fighting for funds to research and find a way to the little girls (and few boys) to live longer, happy and healthier lives.

My Business Lawson Cloud Computing is associated with this charity and my involvement is one that is also personal. Rather than stand here and become overemotional about my gorgeous little niece, Harper, I'll let my father, Dr Lawson, a specialist in the field of Rett Syndrome, take over and update you on the what small steps have been walked and what potential bounds lay close on the horizon. Please welcome my father, Dr Lawson."

Spencer sat down to a round of applause. Without even thinking, Jenna had turned her head and snuggled into Spencer's chest to watch his equally confident father take the stand and go into the science of the company he worked for.

Like his son, Dr Lawson was charming and a little eccentric, but that somehow gave more authenticity to his lecture.

"You tired?" mumbled Spencer to Jenna.

"Fascinated, I'm sorry to say."

"He'll be very flattered when he corners me for your honest critique later."Once we've finished dinner, we've pretty much covered the bare essentials if you want to sneak away for an early night."

"Certainly not. I intend to fulfill my contractual obligations. Besides," she said picking up a folder with an itinerary for the evening. "I believe there's dancing after dessert and cheese and biscuits."

"I'd no idea you were a malingerer," he teased.

"I'd no idea you were such an old man."

He bent his head forward with a mock sneer and before he could help himself, his thick lip and gently caught her bottom lip in his. It was brief, but held the promise of something more. Spencer didn't release immediately. Instead, he watched Jenna pull her lip from the gentle clasp of his teeth.

"I bet the dessert I could offer you would be a lot sweeter than what is on the menu?"

"I have a feeling the cream might be a little salty and sour," replied Jenna.

"You won't know until you try."

"Very true!"

"Does that mean you want to try?" prompted Spencer.

"No," retorted Jenna sharply, "it means I want to dance."

Growling as though it was an unfathomable suggestion, he rose from the table and offered his hand to Jenna. She took it and the dimple of his left cheek popped in and out at pleasure that he'd been able to please her so easily with such a simple gesture.

"I'm glad this music is old school," he whispered as he realized they were the first to take the dance floor.

"Why. Were you going to throw out some of your 80s style break dancing moves?"

Spencer bit his lip from laughing. From the indoor pond partitioning off the head table to the other tables, a giant shell rose and opened to produce a gorgeous iconic jazz singer dressed in the style of a flapper band. Seats emerged along the waterways for the strings and wind and brass instruments to take their positions.

"Looks like you've got me for the first waltz," Jenna teased.

"I'd like to think I have you for every waltz, fox trot or whatever Harlem sound they'll graduate into tonight."

"Was that in our contract?" asked Jenna

"No," he said, "I'm just hoping of all the guys here, I'm the one that'll treat you right and hold your attention all night so you don't go straying."

His brown eyes were piercing and without any note of flippancy. If ever there was a moment to steal a kiss from this modern fairytale she'd fallen in for a night, it was then.

Closing her eyes and tilting her head slightly, she was relieved and delirious when Spencer's, firm soft lips planted on hers. There was no hurry. No tongue diving in to locate her tonsils. It was a sweet, affectionate kiss with the promise of so much more.

"So shall we stay on the dance floor or should I take you home before the clock strikes midnight."

"My slippers aren't made of glass," she whispered, "but now seems as good a time as any to make a move home."

*

With valets lined up, it didn't take long for Spencer's limousine to make its way around to the front. The nesting paparazzi were still waiting.

"Can we ask who you're date is tonight, Mr. Lawson?" shouted one red nosed, overweight journalist who'd been nursing a bottle of whiskey to keep him warm during the last few hours.

"You'd have to ask the young lady," he said shortly, rubbing his hands together. No doubt about it there was a chill in the air tonight that suggested summer

69

may be coming to its natural end.

"So little lady, how long have you been dating Spencer Lawson?"

"We're friends," she smiled. "I know it sounds trite but it's what we are. Spencer does a lot of charity work, I'm studying social work at the university, our paths were bound to cross at some point. I'm privileged to be here contributing to something so important and something that isn't featured prominently in terms of medicine and research."

"Friends aside, are we going to see you and Spencer Lawson hitting the town later this week?"

Jenna laughed.

I should be so lucky, she thought. "I wouldn't be camping out waiting for that photo," she laughed as she hopped in the car.

"I'm super impressed," praised Spencer draping an arm around her shoulder and toying with the shoestring strap.

"Why?"

"That was a pretty ballsy on-record conversation, wasn't it?"

"Truthful, though."

"Truthful in that moment."

The two looked at each other again.

"May I?"

"I'm impressed you feel obligated to ask."

"I'm not a Neanderthal."

Jenna put a finger to his lips. Removing them quickly, she planted her own lips on Spencer's. She'd been waiting to do that since they first met.

Without further invitation, Spencer's hand was already working its way under the shimmering olive-green and gold fabric of Jenna's dress.

"Not like this and not in here!"

"What a little traditionalist you are," he laughed respectfully.

The car pulled up outside Spencer's residences. The chauffeur already had an umbrella open to cover them from the small rain shower that was threatening to break. Once inside the revolving doors, Spencer gave a nod and wink to the receptionist.

As soon as they were in the apartment, Spencer's lips were clamped on Jenna's collarbone as he sucked hard while efficaciously removing her necklace. He flung the simple bejeweled necklace onto the kitchen counter. Spencer could see Jenna's feline-esque eyes note where it landed.

"Don't worry, it's still be yours when you wake," he promised.

"It's not the jewelry that bothers me, it's the fact if it lands in the waste disposal unit and I forget about it, it's going to take forever me to rectify it."

Spencer's hand flew over her mouth.

"Now is really not the time to be talking shop, Ms. King."

Spencer's large thumbed rolled down the shoe string straps of Jenna's gown. Her frame was so narow, the gown effortlessly sank to the floor like a settling autumnal leaf. Realizing she was standing only in her golden bra and lacy thong, she felt very exposed, even if Spencer had dimmed the lights.

Spencer had already struggled to loosen his bow tie and flung his black tails and white waistcoat to the floor. All that was left was for Jenna to unbutton his dress shirt and make her way southward to his trousers.

He offered a hand to her. Unthinkingly she took it, but with the automatic tug, she knew where Spencer was directing her.

"Not in there," she said, shaking her head at the bedroom.

"Jen, don't be foolish. It's clean, comfortable and no one nearly as close to your beauty has ever taken a step into that room."

"You've had dozens of women in that bed."

"But not one was half the lady you are."

"Spencer you've got all the right words-"

"So let me show you all the right moves."

Without giving her time to answer, his hands went forcefully to her shoulders and he flung her back on the king sized wooden bed. The shove was so powerful, Jenna landed with arMs. and legs astray. Spencer wasted no time. He knelt on the end of the bed, being sure to part Jenna's feet and running a firm hand from her throat over her flat stomach to the lining of her underwear. Lifting Jenna's foot one at a time, he kissed each one gently. Moving between her parted legs, he reached for her thong and began slowly peeling it down.

Jenna's hands struggled to cover her modesty in the brightly lit room. Spencer was clearly a man who was tantalized by the physical imagery around him. Peeling the sheer material from one foot, he quickly did the same to the other one. He inhaled her scent deeply form the crotch of her thong.

She saw him do it from the side of her eyes and was flattered that he inhaled so deeply and smiled so sweetly afterward. Discarding the underwear, he parted her legs flat. He examined her public mound. Grinning wolfishly he was thrilled that she'd managed to shave his initials S & L into her trimmed pubic hair.

"You do bestow quite an honor on me tonight."

"I wasn't expecting you to see it," she mumbled, mortified.

"I like it," he said, as he bowed his head for closer examination.

Jenna could feel his warm breath on her pubis. It shivered and quivered. She couldn't pin point exactly what, but she knew she wanted Spencer's hands on it. Lowering his head, Spencer's thumbs parted her soft brown lips. He let his tongue run up and down the length of the crevice. Jenna squirmed on the spot. His tongue let itself amble onto her clit. Jenna could feel herself wriggling and boring down on his tongue to guide him as to how much pressure she required.

"Easy now, tiger," he teased coming up for air. He rested his hand on her mound, leaving his thumb to toy with the clit as he gently brushed the slight growth that defined his initials.

Looking at Spencer, she realized he remained almost fully dressed.

"You going to assist or am I expected to put on a full show?" he asked.

Trying to straighten herself onto her knees, she was able to face Spencer. Although chiseled, his jaw wasn't as square as she initially thought; it was quite boyish with the smattering of stubble and hints of dimples on both cheeks. Closing her eyes to stop her fingers trembling, she slowly undid his dress shirt. Underneath it, she saw thick brown hair curling around his defined pectorals. The hair continued toward his flat stomach. Spencer watched her eyes as they glinted in appreciation of his physique.

Having unbuttoned the shirt, it was left to Spencer to remove his cufflinks and fling his shirt to the floor. His skin was pale, but somehow that excited Jenna's experience of him. Her dark skin contrasting against his paler complexion was the ultimate in sexy.

Spencer's come-to-bed brown eyes lowered as he watched Jenna's hands wrestling the buckle of the belt of his trousers. Her tiny hand moved its way under the trousers and then under the Calvin Klein label of his underpants. Spencer's breath came out as a long whoosh as the coolness of the back of her hand inched its way down his pubic region. He could feel his cock straining at his pants, needing the contact of her hand.

Without waiting, he shoved his trousers and underwear down in a swift movement, revealing a proud eight-inch penis for Jenna to marvel. She gulped at the size of it. Torn between fear and determination, her hand gripped it firmly. She could feel it growing in her hand with the blood pulsating against her palm. He groaned and she knew he wanted it to be in her. The feeling was completely mutual. It was all down to who would make the first move.

Spencer's hand flew to Jenna's throat. Not cruelly, he flung her down on the bed. Instinctively her legs clamped shut. He grinned and crushed his mouth on hers. Preventing her from breathing naturally. She struggled under the sheer weight of Spencer. She wanted the same thing, but his entire body was suffocating her. Eventually he wrestled her till her legs were spread wide enough for him to press the fat purple head against the entrance of her pussy.

She moaned in his mouth.

"Relax," he whispered breaking the kiss. "I don't want to rape you, I want to ravage you."

The hand on her neck relaxed enough for Jenna to

listen and proceed to dip her hips to invite Spencer in. He'd wanted to go slower and gentler, but a man driven by lust doesn't always possess the self-restraint to forbid himself invading a lady so. The thick fat head of his cock slipped into Jenna's slit. She squealed aloud. It had been some time since she'd been sexually active and Spencer wasn't a small guy. He stopped the minute she sounded in pain.

He lay still for a second or two. That her internal vaginal muscles were tight enough to massage Spencer's shaft was driving him insanely horny. He'd no intention of hurting the girl. Taking deep breaths he began to inch his way in and out of her slit. Jenna winced with each new portion, but made no complaint other than the unusual mewl of delight.

Her pussy was gushing so Spencer was in no doubt that she was as needy for him as she was for her. After keeping a gentle reduced speed, Spencer was excited to feel the nails of Jenna's fingers gripping his buttocks, urging him to go deeper. He bucked sporadically like a bronco for a few minutes to let Jenna know just how deep and how rough he could be. Deciding to test his bed partner, his hands gripped her waist like a vice and he rolled on his back, pulling Jenna on top.

Time to see just how badly she wanted his cock. Jenna was on her haunches, hand underneath seeking the thick throbbing muscle to direct it in her pussy. As the head burst through the entrance she threw her hand ack to accommodate the stretch on her pussy. In the same instance, Spencer's hands flew up to unclasp her bra and free her breasts. In the cool air of the flat her nipples hardened like bullets.

"Ride me how you want to," he challenged.

Jenna knew love making clearly was off the cards, but if she only got one shot with this heartthrob, then she'd make the most of it.

Remaining on her haunches, she was able to control the depth of penetration. Occasionally, she'd tease him by taking in and releasing the head of his dick straight away. She'd do it repeatedly – preventing him from experiencing deep penetration. Feeling kinder, she'd bob herself down his shaft inch by inch until he was balls deep. From there, she'd stay still and wriggle on his prick as she ground her clit on his hairy pubic mound. From the teasing, to the lazy fucking it was time for some furious riding and climax.

Adjusting her legs to lower to her haunches, Jenna began to build up a gradual rhythm. As she did, she squeezed her pelvic floor muscles tight. The sensation massaged Spencer's cock, widening it in Jenna's already tight slit. She gasped and began to jerk a little.

Spencer's hands reached up and roughly tugged her bra down. He squeezed her nipple hard and twisted it until she screamed. The reaction of her body was to jolt and buck, permitting Spencer the opportunity to place his hand on her vagina and leave his thumb on her clit As she squeezed his shaft, he pressed and rubbed her slippery clit. Sitting slightly, he let his mouth latch on a free nipple and sucked it hard it the point where his teeth were able to bite hard. That was all that was needed to have her chocolate pussy gushing in orgasm as Spencer shot a massive load of cum deep inside her.

Jenna dropped her head flat onto the damp chest hair of Spencer's heaving torso.

Spencer could sense Jenna wanting to break the calm.

"Don't say a thing," warned Spencer. "Go to sleep, Ms. King," he requested before his own eye lids shut.

Chapter Four

The Egyptian white cotton of the linen felt divine against Jenna's soft skin, but it was the warmth of being cocooned in Spencer's arm. that made this the perfect place to wake up. Keeping her eyes shut, she inhaled deeply to enjoy the smell of the fresh pressed sheets, the aroma of Spencer and the charge of pheromones that flitted round the room. The silence was shattered by an alarm clock.

One of Spencer's long rippled arms reached across Jenna to turn off the alarm. She could feel his stubble brush against her cheek. As she wriggled back into him, she could feel his morning glory pressing against her buttocks.

A sleepy smile spread over his tired face as she teased him.

"Not going to happen, Jenna."

It wasn't a cruel rebuff, but there was something in his tone that hinted she shouldn't attempt to cajole him to change his mind.

"Unfortunately the gym calls and then I've a breakfast meeting and you've got this apartment to clean, which despite your best efforts over the past few weeks, we've managed to undo in a night."

His tone was light, but the distance was unmistakable. Embraced in his arms, Jenna felt more like she was in jail than in a love nest.

"You planning on going home first to get changed before you start work here, or just clean up and take one of my cars back to yours, so you and crash out?"

"You planning on offering me a black coffee before or should I leave?"

"Jenna, don't be like that. You know me and my routines." Spencer bounded out of bed. The muscular thighs were still a delight to feast on, but the sinewy muscles seemed to be preparing to sprint out of her presence. "Besides, you of all people should know where the coffee machine is," he chuckled.

He stopped suddenly when he realized Jenna wasn't laughing.

"It was a joke," he explained, holding his hands up like a child being caught with its hand in the cookie jar.

"Well it wasn't a funny joke."

"Are you getting us a stew, then," he teased.

Jenna was never the violent type and it was rare for her to lose her cool, but she wanted to slap his supercilious face. No wonder the women he normally bedded here were long gone before her early morning arrival, if this was the post sex behavior they were subject to.

"Get it yourself. This place is relatively tidy. I'll do the bedroom and go. I know somewhere that does a better cup of coffee and the company is miles better than what's on offer here."

"Jenna, don't be like that. We had a good night. I actually enjoyed spending time with you, which makes a change, but the world keeps turning. This body won't stay firm and fit if I start skipping sessions at the gym."

"You might want to try investing a little energy into good manners and common decency."

"Have I been anything other than decent or well-mannered to you," asked Spencer directly.

"On the surface yes, but for an actual relationship to occur you need to scratch below the surface, Spencer."

"You're my cleaner."

"Oh right. One doesn't 'scratch the surface' with the hired help to develop a relationship."

"Jenna you are taking this way too personally. If I believed you were nothing more than a maid I wouldn't have taken you out last night and we wouldn't have been sharing a bed afterward."

"Putting your dick in me doesn't mean you've scratched the surface of Jenna King."

"Now you're just being foulmouthed. Cinderella's certainly lost her shine this morning."

Jenna picked up her golden heels. She flung one across the bedroom, deliberately to miss Spencer and land on the bedclothes and followed it in rapid succession with the second one.

"Now who's lacking in manners?" he laughed. "Surely, you aren't going to leave with your paycheck and leave the free outfit behind," he snorted.

Jenna stopped in her tracks. She slowly paced the apartment to recover her jeans, sneakers, polo shirt and apron and dressed herself as each item came into her possession. She dumped the new clothes in the laundry basket. Her hand went to the check sitting on the glass table of the dining room.

She walked in the bedroom for Spencer's full viewing pleasure.

"Why are you behaving like this?" he asked, concerned. "I thought we were having a good time."

"So did I," she said, fluttering her eyelids to stop any tears threatening. "I was paid to have a good time with you for a particular period. I didn't read the small print," she mused reluctantly. "Silly girl that I am."

"Jenna, don't." begged Spencer as he saw her fold the check.

In seconds, eight pieces of paper fluttered to the ground.

"I'd have been thrilled to have gone with you last night for no money. You might think you're behavior this morning is amusing and teasing, but it's insensitive. I don't think I've ever felt so cheap or so used. My friend Kelly thought this was like a real-life romantic comedy.

Well, it's an absolute tragedy, because I've jumped into the role of the lowly hooker with no self-esteem. If you have any decency in you, you'll call Ms. Princely and request a new cleaner and give me a decent reference. I don't believe I've ever let you down professionally."

Spencer looked shamed faced. "Jen, this has got out of hand."

"No," she paused. "Actually maybe you're right. Let's rein it in. Your protocol to keep hired help at an arm's distance appears to be effective. I'll take that one gem of knowledge like this away with me."

She stripped the bed and Spencer watched in horror, knowing if he offered to help it would only make the situation even more awkward. With all her courage, she put fresh sheets on, vacuumed the room and cleaned the bathroom. As she walked out of the bedroom, Spencer reached for her hand. It was so tiny it was like trying to grab grains of sand in the wind.

"Jenna?"

His eyes met hers.

"Good luck with your niece. I hope she hangs on and I hope the researchers keep getting closer to a breakthrough. Never put that little girl at arm's length."

With that, Jenna left the flat, locked the door and burst into a flood of tears.

*

When Jenna stomped into the diner, she wasn't expecting to see her family there,being waited on hand and foot by Kelly, who was using them as an excuse to work slow and enjoy the banter. The expression of her best friend, younger sister, mother and even her toddler niece were of marked disappointment.

"Baby Girl," cooed Jenna's mother, Hannah, giving her a hug.

"I was promised the cat was going to be dragging in something much more impressive than this," snipped Liana.

Even Zada, who spoke very little, looked her aunt up and down and blew a raspberry.

"What, just for once, you couldn't come in looking like a glamorous skank that was on the town all night at some massive charity gala instead of a drab old cleaner?"

Kelly shoved the paper that was spread open on the table of the booth her family shared, showing Jenna the pictures of Spencer and Jenna. The photographs were colored and they did look stunning, but nowhere near as radiant as they'd been in the flesh.

"The clock struck midnight," scowled Jenna, sidling in next to her mother.

The women realized this was something of a taboo topic. They sat in silence awaiting Jenna's guidance on how to discuss what was the event of the decade.

"Correction. The clock struck 5.30 am."

"Oh no you didn't," said Liana, placing her hands over baby Zada's ears.

"Oh yes I did and now I really wish I hadn't."

"What, he awful in bed? Tiny downstairs?" prompted Kelly.

"Girl, it's breakfast and my granddaughter's here. Keep your mind out of the gutter."

"No and No," answered Jenna.

"If he's good in the sack and had a healthy cock, why on earth are you here now?" squealed her mother, laughing.

The three young women caught one another's eyes.

"Settle yourselves," said Hannah. "Baby Zada doesn't know what I'm talking about and we're all women of the world. You think moms can't talk about sex?"

"I think they should talk about sex with their own friends," announced Liana, completely grossed out.

"Let's be mature now," ordered Hannah, slamming her fist on the stainless steel table.

"How'd you end up in the diner at 8 am, when you should be in that pretty British boy's bed right now?"

"He didn't want me there."

"I'm getting her favorite breakfast and taking a break," screeched Kelly.

However, no matter how low her appetite, there was no way Jenna was able to resist the lure of the waffles with fresh cream, banana, walnuts and caramel sauce.

"What happened?" started Kelly.

"The night was indescribably perfect. Spencer's father, mother and two older brothers are all in the medical professional, high up in their fields of expertise. Turns out Spencer just didn't have the same knack. Not that he's thick. Chatting with his father, he excelled academically and got into computers and literally made himself a billionaire."

"Yeah, but mummy and daddy had the money to give him the education he needed and I bet they had the network connections to get him in his field," countered Kelly.

"I'm not saying that he doesn't come from a privileged background. I'm not saying that his family doesn't have a secure financial background to enable him to follow the course he wanted in life. What I'm saying is he got out there and used his talents and did his own thing rather than rely on his surname and the reputation of his relatives."

"Nothing wrong there," said Hannah.

"He accumulates his fortune and check this out. He has a niece born with Rett Syndrome."

"Ahhhhhh", the table harmonized in union.

"Guys do you know what Rett syndrome is?"

The women shook their heads.

"Uh-uh," said Zada.

"At least she's being honest," giggled Jenna.

"It's a genetic neurological disorder. Messes up their bodies and well, Spencer's niece may not get to see thirty. He doesn't have the medical know-how to fight this horrible condition, but he spends the majority of his time and puts an excessive amount of his earnings into promoting and trying to advance research on the condition."

"I'm waiting to hear the part where he turns into an ogre," sighed Jenna's mother.

"He didn't turn into an ogre, mum."

Hannah could tell from the sound of her voice that he had. Her hand went to her daughter's face and she cupped her cheek and turned her toward her. Looking into her mothers almost black eyes, Jenna wanted to place her face in her mother's lap and weep. She didn't want to feel cheap. She didn't want to feel used. She didn't want to feel like a whore and she didn't want to feel like she would never amount to anything more than a nothing, a flibbity jibbit in

89

Spencer's eyes.

"You're not that, baby girl," her mother murmured in her ear, not needing her daughter to talk.

"You want to keep it in, that's fine. You want to share, we've got all the time in the world - even Kelly here."

"I was the idiot, mum. You'd think I'd grow up or learn from my past mistakes but it doesn't happen. He's just another charming knight on a white horse who I thought might come and rescue me."

The table was silent. The grownups were fully au fait with Jenna's history.

"Still, in fairness, I suppose he did charge in and rescue me. I earned $1000 for being his date."

"Best news ever!" said Liana punching a fist in the air.

"Hush your mouth," snapped Hannah.

Liana never argued with her mother.

"I tore it up and threw it away. I'm not an escort. I slept with him because I wanted to, but when I saw that check on the table it seemed to make a mockery of me and my morals. I run into those good looking, charming men that can provide me financial stability, but not one of them wants the fairytale happily-ever-after with me. What's that say about me as a person?"

"It says you haven't met the right man," said her mother serenely.

"It says you're the kind of girl that merely needs a helping hand now and again because you're so busy conquering the world as a woman of independent means," stated Kelly positively.

"It says you aren't the kind of girl who needs to be rescued. Where exactly could Prince Charming find a place in your life, and why would he want to? Your university fees are paid up, you've got a job, you're devoted to your family and you study full time. Where in that schedule does Prince Charming get a slice of your life? You don't need rescuing. You don't have time for Mr Right, that's why you never meet him."

Liana's assessment was the most hurtful, but Jenna knew that was because it was the most truthful.

"I don't want to be rescued," she snapped. "I would like to be respected and valued."

"You are," insisted Kelly.

"I know. And you guys mean the world to me, but I'd like it if just one man could see my potential. What I have to offer a relationship."

"One man did," grumbled Liana.

"Forget that man," snapped Hannah. "Why is your tongue so loose this morning? Liana. That Leon did nothing good for our Jenna."

"That's not strictly true," interjected Jenna.

"He was a bad influence. You've walked away from him now. We've all walked away from him now."

Jenna chewed her lip. Leon had let her walk away from him. He'd been adamant she do so. He'd wanted her to walk away, because Leon did see her as a Princess that deserved a fairytale ending. The problem was Leon was the frog, not the prince, and there wasn't much he could offer her in the way of a happy ending behind bars.

"He was a small time crook who led you astray."

"Mum, he led me to New York University."

Hannah sat still; her lips were in a thin line. She hated Leon's name in conversation. In the kindness of her daughter's eyes she saw compassion, loyalty and what she knew was puppy love.

"And he led himself to jail. Best advice he gave you was to stay away from him. For God sakes, heed it – it's the only sensible thing that ever came out of that boy's troublesome mouth. And if this posh British man is going to treat you like a pay-as-you-go prostitute, leave the agency and find another job. Come back and work here with Kelly. It's honest work and maybe the temptation of these fairytale endings will be knocked out of that foolish head of yours for good."

The remainder of the meal was a somewhat restrained affair. Kelly was relieved when she was able to return from her break. She squeezed her best friend's shoulder. Even Zada knew better than to throw a tantrum, when faced with the high chair. Liana and Jenna exchanged frightened and half-amused looks.

"You know, mom--" started Liana.

"Not another word, I said," she snapped.

Liana said nothing. When they got into the flat, the girls watched their mother head straight to the bedroom. The girls sat in silence pretending to watch a cartoon with Zada. Eventually they could hear their mother dozing.

"She's working tonight?" asked Jenna.

Liana nodded.

"But that's not what's got her in a mood."

Jenna shrugged.

"Then what?"

"You ever tell mom I gave you this, you and I are through, FOREVER."

Jenna reached to take the envelope from Zada's hand.

"It's Leon," she mumbled.

"Isn't he due out soon?" whispered Liana.

Chapter Five

"Ms.. King. I wasn't expecting to see you so soon."

Jenna sat down opposite her employee's desk.

"Do you know why you've been called in?"

"I spoke with Mr. Lawson over the weekend and we agreed that perhaps we need to reassess my roster."

"Well if you did, he made no mention of it to me."

"He has asked me to deposit an additional $1000 into your back account for this week's pay."

Jenna's back stiffened in the chair. It was like ice had been breathed into the normally snug office.

"I thought it an odd request, but when I found these pictures of the two of you cavorting at the Rett Syndrome Charity Gala, he informed me you stepped in last minute as a date for the evening and he wished to pay you for your time. Apparently you forgot to collect your check the following shift."

Discreet till the very end, thought Jenna. "I believe I did. It was thoughtful of him to deposit it with you."

"That particular duty doesn't really come under your normal routine."

"It was an emergency. It appeared Mr. Lawson had

no one to help out, and as a good client I thought I could assist him, if possible."

"You do realize what kind of an agency we are don't you, Ms.. King."

"Or course," said Jenna firmly but politely.

"Because we aren't an undercover escort agency."

"If you're implying for one second that I would lower myself-"

"Please keep control, Ms. King. I was implying nothing of the kind. I have always found you to be of high character and good standing, hence your employment at the agency. Surely you understand from my point of view, I couldn't afford to have the time, money and history I've invested in Supreme Cleaning Services become tarnished over a one night fling or a short term affair."

Jenna was preparing to defend herself when Ms. Princely rotated the newspaper gossip section to her. A photo taken at 2 am showed Spencer and Jenna entering Spencer's apartment block, a photo taken just after 6 am had a picture of a half-dressed disheveled Jenna leaving the building in her Supreme Cleaning Services Uniform.

"That's not what it looks like," she said quietly.

"There may be a perfectly reasonable story behind it and I wouldn't question your integrity if you confided it to me. The problem is Jenna, that photo is what it looks like."

"I don't want our male client base that has the finances and taste to indulge in activities similar to what I'm sure was the perfectly innocent date you embarked on Friday night, believing that may become something we offer permanently, as an additional extra. Our high standards revolve around cleaning services, not the bedroom services our employees may or may not want to supply."

"Am I out of a job then?"

"No. Not at all."

Jenna's chest loosened considerably. She found the imaginary chokehold on her neck disappear.

"He specifically asked for this incident not to go on your records or for you to be disciplined and I'll respect Mr. Lawson's wish there. I cannot, however, indulge his whim that you continue working for him. He feels you are the only trustworthy maid in New York, but he'll soon learn there are others that are as trustworthy as you but a lot less alluring."

Jenna struggled hard to gulp down a sob. Sounded like Spencer wanted to make up, not break up. Now this was becoming a fairytale and Ms. Princely was the wicked witch.

"Where will I be working then?"

"Here. Once your classes are finished, you'll clean the offices in the evening Monday to Saturday."

"Actually. That's not so good for me. My sister attends night classes and—"

"Your working here won't stop her education," said Ms. Princely curtly.

"No, but I need to babysit my niece so my sister's able to go to school."

"Don't look shocked Jenna. We aren't anti family values here. I understand your predicament. It looks like you're going to need to use Mr. Lawson's $1000 bonus to purchase a portacot for you to clean the premises while babysitting."

Jenna put her head in her hands. There really was no comeback to that.

*

Jenna had no idea why she was shivering when the sun was radiating and there wasn't a cloud in the sky. The building in front of her didn't look particularly foreboding. All things considered, the minimal security prison appeared quite pleasant from the outside.

"It's going inside that's the problem."

Checking the visitor pass still clenched tight in her sweaty fist, she made her way to reception to undergo the formal and unwelcoming process required to visit an inmate.

As they searched her handbag, insisted she fill out reams of paperwork and provide identification, all she could think about was how most people visiting Long Island were rich and visiting the Hamptons - not seeing ex-boyfriends serving time.

Sent forward, on sight of Leon, Jenna thought she might rush up to him and throw her arMs. round his neck. He shook his head, reading her eyes carefully. With two fingers, he tapped the opposite end of the table indicating she should sit.

When he smiled, Jenna's entire body relaxed. The even white teeth and plump lips stretched over his defined stubbled jaw line. He had a trimmed black moustache and beard and looked impeccable groomed in his drab prison uniform.

"Hey girl, how you doing?" his voice was deeper than she remembered.

Jenna found herself studying Leon quite carefully. He

99

was a monster at six foot five. His chocolate brown skin was flawless. He seemed fit and akin to a brick wall. There wasn't a scratch on him.

"What are you worrying about, girl? You know I can look after myself. You don't need to be putting me down first on your list of social work charity cases," he grinned.

She laughed genuinely. "You look huge."

"Ain't nothing to do but work out in the gym when you're trying to stay on the right path and get out on good behavior."

"How's that working out for you?"

"I told you not to mind me," he chided. "Told you that a while back. Don't be worrying yourself about how I'm doing."

"And I've respected that. You asked me to visit."

"Yeah I did. Thought I should put you in the picture. Something odd happened in the last couple of days."

"Tell me about it," she said under her breath, thinking of her own sudden change in life. Her frustrated niece being confined to a playpen each evening while Jenna cleaned the Supreme Cleaning Services Offices building as a punishment for breaking the employer – employee code.

"I don't know how exactly, but somehow I got roped into seeing this weird sounding, pretty boy I'd never even heard of. British, I bet. Don't know what strings he can pull, but me declining to see him wasn't an option."

Jenna's heart sank.

"What'd he look like?"

"White. Tall. Broad. Slim, but not skinny. Curly hair with dimples. Looked younger than he probably was. Good-looking if you like pale skin and dark features. Bit pretty for my taste – maybe not for yours, Jen."

They sat silently.

"You know him?" enquired Leon.

"I do. What did he want?"

"He was nosing around. He never said he was a cop, but he acted like a man that expected answers. Are you in trouble, girl?"

Jenna shook her head.

"No."

"Cause if you are, the past year and a bit of my doing time has been a complete waste of time."

"I'm not in any trouble. My grades are good. I'm

holding down a job. Mum, me, Liana and little Zada are surviving nicely."

"Your mum still hate my guts?"

Jenna rolled her eyes.

"Nah, that's a good thing Jen. Keeps you focused on the right path. Means when you graduate you'll stop people like me falling in with the wrong crowd when they're too young to know better."

Jenna's hand reached over and squeezed his. Their eyes met and in seconds, they exchanged a look of shared youths and growing up. Leon released her hand abruptly.

"He was nosing about your university fees. How they were paid? When were they paid up until? That sort of thing."

"What'd you say?"

"I went on to say I had no idea because I don't know you no more, but he'd done his background checks. He knew we had a history, even knew we were neighbors. I told him it wasn't any of his goddamn business."

Jenna was silent. She knew the essence of Spencer and he was a man who was determined to achieve what he set out to do. He may not have a cure for Rett

Syndrome, but it didn't impinge on his focus or determination. Locating how Jenna's university fees were paid was small stuff to a man in Spencer's position. He'd have got an answer from Leon. Leon's brawn was no match for Spencer's intellect.

"You put me in the yard with this jumped up playboy in his posh suit and I'd wipe the floor with him, but that wasn't an option. I had a feeling he could be dangerous."

"He wouldn't hurt you," assured Jenna.

"Yeah he would. I think to protect you, he'd hurt anyone," mused Leon. "I told him the truth. My uncle pays your fees. He runs a legitimate garage. He's your godfather and he feels obligated to. And that is the truth, Jenna. Any dealings I had with my uncle and the small petty crime I was into was between me and him. It has nothing to do with the motor repair shop."

"Your uncle does it as a favor to you, though. And to owe you that favor, you must've helped him out in ways that weren't strictly by the book."

"That ain't your business, girl. Your business is to study hard, stay afloat and do something with your life. You keep doing that I won't break my promise to you."

Jenna felt a tear at the corner of her eye. She missed Leon. She loved him, but she wasn't in love him. She just loved the way he cared about her. The way he saw the best in her. That he thought she'd have a better chance in life if he was absent from hers forever.

"I'll keep doing that," she assured him. "And you'll keep your promise to me."

"I will. I'll be out of here soon enough. Finished up my apprenticeship in here so I can get myself a proper job with a steady wage and work my way up. Keep my head down and my nose clean and you won't ever find yourself near one of these places again. You won't have to hear any stories round the neighborhood about me becoming a regular visitor of these kinds of facilities."

"That sounds fine."

"You gotta work hard too, Jen. Do your best to stop kids like me picking this route in life. Then everything will have been worth it, right?"

She nodded.

"I told you what I thought you should know about this prissy Brit. You oughta know what game he's playing at, and those kinds of stunts can only come from a man with a plan. Be aware. Get yourself out of here now. Scoot, girl."

Before he could stop her, Jenna leaned over and kissed his forehead chastely.

"It wasn't all bad, was it, Leon?"

"Jenna, when we were little, too young to know how poor we were, too silly to know what we were missing out on, we had the best time ever. Trouble is people like us don't get to keep their childhoods. Father's walking out, drink and drug habits rife in the family, scrounging for food and money – you can't keep your innocence in that environment.

I thought crime was the way out. Seemed joining a gang was a quick fix. Thought it'd get us the best in life. Didn't get us anywhere. You saved my life though, Jen. I was busy trying to play the big man to look after you and I didn't realize you were looking after yourself. You had your head buried in a book. I thought you may as well have had your head in the clouds. You picked the hard path, but it's getting you to a better place and for what it's worth – you saved my life, Jenna. I can follow your example. Took me longer, but I see yours is the right way, the best way. I'm proud I know you."

Jenna screwed her eyes tight, knowing it'd stop the waterfall of tears.

"But Jen," started Leon as she made her way to the exit door. "It definitely wasn't all bad. When we were little kids, we had the best time ever and growing up with you was a privilege. Took it for granted at the time, but those memories are the best for me. You make better memories now, even if it is with some wealthy white boy."

Going through the mundane process of pat downs, security checks, retrieving personal goods and signing out, when she finally stepped out into the light Jenna could feel the sun on her skin and see the beautiful brilliant blue of the sky.

She had got out. She'd got out on her own and she was proud of the woman she was.

*

Jenna groaned as she approached the Supreme Cleaning Services building. Her rucksack was weighing her down and Zada was less than impressed being carted round New York in a rickety red pram in the rush hour.

"I'm sorry, baby girl," she apologized as she used the fob to open the main entrance to the building. Immediately as she was on the premises, the security alarm started. Zada was screaming. Jenna was punching the code into the panel. It mightn't silence Zada, but at least it did halt the siren. She sat on the stairs, close to Zada's pram.

"I'm really hoping this won't be forever, angel," she cooed. Rocking the pram a bit, Zada's cries softened to whimpers.

"Shall Aunty Jenna start from the top down or work her way bottom up," voiced Jenna aloud.

The quiet of the vacant building at night was quite eerie.

"Top down, I think. That's where I left the cleaning materials last night."

She pushed the pram to the elevator and waited for the bell to ring to signal its arrival.

Hopping in, it glided quickly to the 26th floor.

"Thank God, Ms. Princely only leases three of these floors or you and I would never make it home. Not that I'm looking forward to the subway journey back."

Jenna fling off backpack. Yes, the cot was lightweight, portable and compact but it was still cumbersome in the backpack. It sprung to life with little assistance from Jenna.

"In you go," she said, placing her niece inside.

She took a handful of toys out of her pack and flung

them in the cot for Zada to play with. Kissing her niece softly, she inhaled the scent of fresh soap and clean clothes.

The arrangement was hideous for the toddler but she made no complaint. It wasn't as if she could even wear her headphones while working, lest Zada need her immediate attention.

"Okay, keep busy and Aunty will do her best to get you out of here as quickly as possible."

It wasn't a solid promise. Jenna was glad Zada was fully comprehensive of the English language. With prim Ms. Princely as her direct supervisor, Jenna wasn't in a position where she could cut corners and afford to be careless in her cleaning duties. Ms. Princely had an eye for dust and Jenna suspected she'd be giving her the white glove treatment for her first few days of work.

Having wiped the computer monitors, sanitized the telephones, tidied and polished the desks and emptied the bins, Jenna knew which came next. The sound of the raucous vacuuming would drive Zada mad. She popped some candy in Zada's mouth knowing her sister and mother would be furious at her for giving the toddler such sugary treats so late at night. Looping the headphones over her neck, she placed the headphones from her iPod into Zada's ears. Scrolling to Zada's favorite play list, she double-checked the volume control to ensure no damage could be done to the youth's sensitive ears. Jenna stood back and watched with genuine joy as Zada clapped her time in rhythm to the music.

"You look like you might want one of those for yourself one day," drawled a familiar voice in an unfamiliar setting.

Jenna found herself screeching in fright, which in turn had Zada screaming her lungs out. Spencer's hands flew to his ears to block the noises.

"What are you doing here?"

"What are you doing here?" he mouthed the question back in mute.

Jenna tore the headphones from Zada's tiny ears and lifted her to her hip. She jiggled the babe on her hip to calm her and whispered sweet nothings in her ears. It appeared to have very little effect on calming her.

"Why don't you let me have a turn," proposed Spencer, hoping his voice was deep enough to undercut Zada's high pitched squeals.

"What would you know about little girls—"

Jenna stopped herself from finishing the sentence. She wished she could've bitten the tip of her tongue off. Spencer clearly had a lot to do with his niece, if his recent trip abroad had anything to do with it.

She passed Zada to him. Zada's thick little hands looped around his neck. Spencer's beautiful long lashes closed as he smothered Zada's face in kisses pretending to kiss away all her tears. She giggled and looked adoringly at him.

"Sorry I gave you and Aunty a fright, beautiful little girl. It must've seemed like the big bad wolf had come creeping up to spy on you when it was just a friend."

"Friends shouldn't be sneaky in nature," said Jenna sharply.

"Tweet, tweet, tweet," mocked Spencer, "someone's been singing like a canary."

"Someone's been keeping an eye on an old friend to warn her to stay away from a wolf in sheep's clothing."

Spencer smiled wolfishly and Jenna despised herself for being charmed.

"What are you doing here?" she asked again.

"What are you doing here?"

"Stop answering questions with questions Spencer's – it's childish."

Spencer had given Zada a key ring with a plush brightly colored monster on it that made an array of cute noises when squeezed in an appropriate place. Transfixed, Spencer was able to lower her in the portacot to continue the adult conversation without interruption.

"I came here to find out exactly what you are doing here when I didn't ask for you to be relocated."

Jenna looked dumbfounded.

"Close your mouth, you'll catch flies."

"I'm here because of some photos that were all across the tabloids from that charity function I attended as your guest."

"Date," corrected Spencer.

"Guest," insisted Jenna. "If you hadn't insisted I take the check it might've been a date, but you were quick to remind me where to find it the following morning, thus making it a job."

"And you were quick to tear it up in front of my eyes, which in my reckoning means we were on a date."

"Yes, but then you insisted that you transfer the funds into my personal account thereby putting the final nail in the coffin and confirming it was nothing more than a duty of service."

"I was under the impression it might help with your university fees, but I can see I was off on that particular hunch."

"Spencer, what freak has a private investigator on my case to unravel the mystery of how my university tuition is funded?"

"The kind of billionaire freak who wants a second date."

"Do you realize how warped that sounds?"

"I wanted to know that truth," he said honestly.

"You only had to ask."

"It may have been safer doing it this way."

"Meaning what?"

"Meaning look at your background, Jenna. Your university fees are paid for by a childhood sweetheart's uncle. This random man is paying your fees and he has no real connection with you. He's doing it because he's obligated to his nephew – your ex. It's dirty money."

"It's not dirty money," she turned on him harshly. "The motor shop is legitimate. It doesn't launder money and the man that runs it has a reputable, established practice so don't go poking your nose in where it doesn't belong, Spencer Lawson."

"Maybe you need to wise up and start poking your nose in. There's something amiss here Jenna. No one gets a free ride. Do you think at some point down the line, Leon or his uncle won't be calling on a favor, reminding you who paid for you to get to university?"

The thought hadn't occurred to Jenna. It was evil and she didn't want to think that of Leon, but a voice deep inside her told her it wasn't out of the realms of possibilities.

"And what's the solution, then."

Spencer sat on a desk and stretched his feet out. He let his eyes caress Jenna's for a long time.

"Let me pay the tuition. I'll reimburse Leon's uncle for what he's paid so far and cover the remainder of your fees. That way the money is clean and you don't owe anyone anything. It can really be a fresh start for you."

"Spencer, how is doing that any different to what I'm doing now?"

"Because it's me."

"You? The man that can't hold down a relationship. The man that's all money and focus with no time for passion and relationships."

"That's the kind of man Jenna, who won't be playing games with you. Toying with ties and loyalties, calling in favors isn't what I do. I'm in a financial position where I don't need to call in favors. Your fees won't even mark my bank balance. It's a business transaction. A charitable act. There's no emotion or feelings included to tarnish the set up."

"Don't you get it, Spencer?"

"Get what?"

"I don't want to be a charity. I don't want to be some girl from the wrong side of the tracks that you help. I want to mean something to you. I want to belong to you. I want your investment to be an emotional one in me, not a financial one in my future."

The room was quiet. The raspy breathing of the two adults reverberated down the corridor.

"I never asked for you to be relocated, Jenna."

"I know, Spencer. Ms. Princely saw the spread from the paparazzi in the tabloids. She had a bizarre idea that the exclusive clientele may be under the impression we offer services other than cleaning. She didn't want people assuming she was the madam of a high class escort agency that ran under the guise of a domestic cleaning service."

The two of them laughed at the idea.

"You were my contingency plan," confessed Spencer.

"Truly?"

"Yeah."

"I got first refusal – how flattering."

"I got the text on my way from London saying my date for the charity had been cancelled. I did the math and realized you'd be in the flat when I arrived. I figured if I went in on charm offensive with a whopping great check then there was every chance you wouldn't reject me."

"You know. I'd have accepted the invite even if it hadn't come with a check. I'd have accepted the invite if you asked me as soon as you walked in the door."

"I figured as much," he grinned lazily.

"Every girl dreams of being a princess for a night. The whole Cinderella scenario, but you know what was so perfect about that date?"

Spencer didn't bother arguing over whether it was a date or not.

"I wasn't pretending to be a princess. I was a princess. I didn't feel like a fish out of water. I didn't feel out of my league. I didn't feel like I was

115

struggling to socialize. I wasn't battling to keep up. I was part of the scene and the scene flowed so easily with you next to me. It was a perfect night. It's a shame Prince Charming turned into a frog the following morning."

Spencer blushed and on his pale skin it was evident he was mortified when thinking over his behavior.

"It's like you said. I'm good with money and computers, but women are something else. If I'd woken up to some investment bonds or a laptop I'm sure I'd have been charm personified, but I didn't. I woke up next to a princess and I realized I'd crossed every line and every boundary I'd ever set myself. I mean if anything, the awkwardness of this entire situation does reinforce my belief that you don't mix business with pleasure."

"Least we've established that," confirmed Jenna, trying to keep her voice steady.

"Have we?"

"You said," reminded Jenna.

"I understand that my hiring the PI and running police checks - which all came back clean I might add- were well over the top, but I was being serious when I said I wanted that second date. I need to get to know you better. I want to get to know you better. I might find the answers out better if I do it firsthand rather than hiring someone to do all the ground work for me."

"That is kind of the point of dating. Putting in the legwork to see if a couple can work or not."

"So are you willing to go on a second date with me?" his smile was half arrogant, but Jenna could see the hope in his eyes.

"We're very different people, Spencer."

"I know all this. I can't relate to your world at all. My mum and dad have been married forever, my family is well to do in the medical field, I had a privileged upbringing, the finest education, handshakes and employment opportunities from all the right people and I'm immersed in that social class. It's a world you've never been a part of and maybe you won't want to be a part of it, but I'd love it if you were open minded enough to give it a try."

Jenna closed her eyes and thought hard. Leon was right. She had to move forward and upward and make changes. Dating billionaire Spencer Lawson would be the first step in that process.

"You've got your second date, Mr. Lawson."

Spencer grabbed her by the wrist and pulled her to him tight. The force of his vice like grip was threatening and sexy. As he bowed his head for his lips to meld with hers she could feel the warmth sizzling between them. Tilting his pelvis forward, Jenna had an idea of how badly Spencer wanted this second date.

Jenna struggled free.

"Oh, Mr. Lawson?"

"Yes, Ms.. King."

"A second date does not constitute you and me sharing Zada's juice in the portacot while I'm at work."

"No?"

"No. I suggest you get your thinking cap on and come up with something more suitable."

"I'll take that as my marching orders then," he replied, giving Jenna brief salute.

"I'll be waiting to hear from you."

Spencer meekly turned to the elevator and waved goodbye.

"Spencer?" called Jenna.

His finger hit the door open button. She ran forward and kissed him more passionately on the lips.

"I really can't wait."

He cheekily bit her bottom lip, forcing her to pull back. As she caught a hint of blood on her lip she watched the let the lift begin its descent.

Chapter Six

Spencer Lawson was not accustomed to not being in control and the current situation didn't sit well with him. He wasn't exactly sure how long he'd been staring aimlessly at the computer screen monitor. He wasn't even sure in his mind exactly what task he'd set himself to do in his multibillion IT company because the only thing on his mind at the moment, was Jenna King.

She should've been nothing more than a faceless cleaner in his New York penthouse but the motivated, family-oriented Brooklyn born and bred NYU student had caught his attention, against his better judgment. Unlike the other women he normally dated, Jenna was refreshingly honest and warm-hearted. Spencer was unused to unbridled emotions and enthusiasm and was charmed by Jenna.

After some unfortunate photos, her employer decides to relocate Jenna, to prevent anything indiscreet happening between the lovers. Jenna now worked evenings cleaning an office building and Spencer was left with a pleasant, middle-aged cleaner doing a flawless job with his apartment.

But being deprived of Jenna as his cleaner, meant spending time with her was almost impossible, with their clashing schedules. The easiest way to resolve the problem was to insist Jenna be relocated back to his apartment, but Spencer knew it was a pompous request.

Shutting his eyes, he felt a pang of guilt. If he demanded Jenna be reinstated, his new cleaner Mrs. Kozak's abilities may come under scrutiny. He didn't want her out of a job or thinking that Spencer didn't appreciate the work she did. Nor was Spencer going to sit down with Mrs. Kozak to explain his personal motivations, either.

Ms. Princely, the director of Supreme Cleaning Services, who provided Spencer with his cleaners, was a formidable woman. The association of a pretty cleaner with a British billionaire playboy was unwanted attention for her company. He respected that and knew professionally the value of an impeccable reputation, thus talking her round to his way of thinking was a somewhat daunting task.

Sometimes throwing money at a problem just doesn't yield the magical solution you want, thought Spencer. *I could, of course, hire Jenna directly. Increase her wage, give her back her hours and bypass Ms. Princely completely. It would be a win-win situation.*

But would it, he thought.

He let his dark brown eyes scan his desk to find the newspaper that had the incriminating photos of a glammed up Jenna entering his residence and a less than groomed Jenna in her Supreme Cleaning Services uniform sneaking out of his premises the following morning. To him, she looked beautiful in both pictures.

"This paper is days old," said Spencer aloud. "Why

do I still even have it on my desk, let alone opened on that page?" He knew the answer, but did not want to admit it to himself.

It was Jenna who was suffering the most. The arrangement had a severe impact on the quality of Jenna's life and her family's – and that wasn't fair. The shift from selfishness to actually considering what Jenna was going through was the incentive Spencer needed. He placed a far greater value on pride than money. Buying Ms. Princely's compliance would be easy but swallowing his pride and asking her to help him was a greater sacrifice.

Jenna didn't deserve this. She hadn't asked to be his date. She hadn't asked to be photographed. She hadn't asked to be the object of Spencer's growing attraction. She shouldn't be the one to be punished.

Sucking in his cheeks and making a whistling sound with his pursed plump lips, Spencer braced himself for the phone call. He ran a hand down his hollowed cheekbones, shook his head, dialed Supreme Cleaning Services, and asked to be put through to Ms. Princely.

"Mr. Lawson, how can I help you?" asked Ms. Princely; cool, but friendly.

"It's not about how you can help me, but how you can help Jenna."

There was silence on the line.

"Why do I get the feeling my helping Jenna is going

to help you?"

Spencer didn't respond.

"Is there a problem with Mrs. Kozak?" prompted Ms. Princely, knowing she'd given Spencer one of her top cleaners.

"Of course not. She's perfect and I've no complaints about her work."

"If that's the case, I suggest you let me look after my own employees."

"Under normal circumstances, I would, but I feel responsible for Jenna's current predicament."

"Jenna's an adult and can take responsibility for her own actions."

"I know that," said Spencer, slightly annoyed. "Jenna didn't ask for the paparazzi to follow her or track her movements during the time spent with me. She wouldn't have even been aware that came with the territory. Had she known the potential consequences, I'm sure she'd have been a lot more discreet. It was unfortunate she was photographed in her uniform."

"It was unfortunate for her and for me."

"I know. We have a saying in England, 'Today's news is tomorrow's fish and chips paper'."

"I'm aware of it," said Ms. Princely drily.

"Then you know this will blow over. It was tabloid fodder the next day, but nobody cares who I date – certainly not long term."

"That's not true, though, is it, Mr. Lawson. If nobody cared who you were linked to, those photographs would never have been printed."

She has you there, old boy, thought Spencer, giving Ms. Princely a private point in their war of words.

"But think of all the women I'm photographed with. I bet you couldn't remember who I was photographed with a two weeks ago, let alone two months ago."

Spencer did have a reputation as a ladies' man.

"This call to me then, is to tell me that your evening with Jenna King was nothing more than a one-night stand?" goaded Ms. Princely.

"No, it most certainly isn't," barked Spencer. "This is to say that I can understand you wanting to put distance between myself and Jenna, in respect to your company, but the current regime of having her working nights while babysitting seems unfair. I know she's grateful how accommodating you are regarding the situation surrounding her family, but it seems a punishment. I was hoping you might reconsider her work placement."

"And put her back with you?"

"Ideally yes, but realistically, I see that wouldn't

work and isn't feasible for a number of reasons. Surely, you must have other clients on your books that may perhaps have more reasonable hours that fit in with her studies and family commitments."

"Mr. Lawson, you sound as if you care."

Spencer was silent.

"I don't like to see anyone inconvenienced because of my status and I feel responsible for what's happened to Jenna. If you did reconsider your position on this and possibly could find another client with better fitting hours for Jenna, could you at least discuss it with her?"

"Jenna didn't put you up to this?"

"No. She needs the job and is grateful you didn't fire her for breaching the terms of her contract by dating me."

"I suppose we all make errors of judgment," said Ms. Princely softly. "Especially when bedazzled by Prince Charming."

"I wouldn't go that far."

His rich, baritone and English accent was irresistible, but Ms. Princely wasn't going to let him know that. He'd charmed her; not because he was well spoken but because he sounded as though he valued in Jenna the same attributes that she did.

"I'll see what I can do."

"I'd be grateful," concluded Spencer graciously.

*

Spencer gave it a night before deciding to venture into Brooklyn. Thanks to the earlier work of his private investigator, he already had Jenna's home address. He arranged for a driver to take him to her two-bedroom apartment by 7pm.

The driver would wait. Spencer wondered if his chauffeur had any concerns about being in this neighborhood while he went to woo Jenna. He hated becoming emotionally involved in other people's lives. Keeping people at arm's length resulted in keeping his heart safe. He didn't want to become attached to other people whose lives he couldn't improve; it made him feel powerless.

His three-year-old niece was a perfect example of this. She had been born with Rett Syndrome, which had no cure and limited her life span. It flummoxed the family. Apart from Spencer, everyone else was in the medical field, but no one was able to help her or prolong her life. It was too heart breaking for Spencer. His billions couldn't save her and the frustration gnawed at him daily. Losing his niece was his greatest and most inevitable fear.

Spencer was good at distancing himself; this was especially true of how he treated the hired help: always with respect, but as nothing more than humans carrying out a job for him. Spencer didn't like to think of their home lives or whether they were married with children or perhaps if they had relatives in a similar position to his own. He had enough to deal with in his own life without someone else's burdens.

Yet Jenna was a woman who wasn't prepared to let Spencer stand on the outskirts of what people had to offer. She'd dragged him into her life just by being herself and he was enamored.

Groaning inwardly, he observed his driver, Graham White. "Think you'll be alright here Graham?" he asked awkwardly.

He could see the middle-aged man stiffen in surprise at the question. His blue eyes looked confused as he assessed his boss.

"Certainly, Mr. Lawson."

"I don't know this neighborhood," said Spencer gruffly. "I wondered if you felt the same. Perhaps you wanted to go to cafe or take a drive somewhere familiar and I could call you when I need to be picked up, something like that." Spencer knew he was rambling. He didn't want to offend the man by suggesting he couldn't look after himself but he didn't want to seem uncaring.

"You've a state of the art machine, sir," reminded the bemused driver. "This Hummer has alarms, bullet proof glass and an armored body. I'm probably safer in here than in my own home."

Spencer flushed embarrassed. That was true. The pimped up Hummer was a beast. "Sure."

"Mr. Lawson?"

"Yes, Graham."

"I really appreciate the offer, though. It means a lot."

Spencer could feel his chest increasing with a mixture of pleasure and pride. "No, problem."

With a spring in his step, he made his way into what appeared, to him to be a ghetto. The elevator of the high-rise apartment block was broken. Fortunately, Jenna was only on the fourth floor.

"It must be a real pain at night carting a baby and a pram up here after school and work," thought Spencer.

He knocked on the door. There was movement behind the door and Spencer sensed someone was checking the peephole. He waited as chains were unfastened and bolts unlocked. Jenna opened the door with her niece cradled in her arms.

"What on Earth are you doing in this neck of the woods?"

"Can I answer that question when I've come inside?" responded Spencer.

Jenna stood back and let Spencer walk through. He noted she was quick to lock up once he was in. The place was cute – homely and clean – but he still had an urge to grab Jenna by the hand and whisk her and baby Zada back to his home where he knew they'd be safe and sound. Jenna, however, didn't look as though she was fazed. He had a feeling if he acted on impulse he'd end up offending her greatly.

"Guess I owe you a thank you?"

Spencer shook his head, "Ms. Princely was always going to calm down. I hope I sped up the process."

"Can I fix you a drink? Hot or cold? Soft or hard?"

There was something in her manner that beguiled Spencer, warm, welcoming, and completely composed in an environment that could never be controlled. That was what Spencer admired. Jenna was able to deal with what cropped up as it happened. Spencer liked to cover all bases so there were no disruptions in his life; it was a luxury he could afford.

"What are the chances of me getting a decent cup of tea here?"

"About the same as you getting a glass of Dom Perignon."

He laughed. "Touché."

"I promise I'll get some in for you for next time," said Jenna. "Tea that is, not champagne." Jenna placed a glass of red wine in front of him. "Let me get this munchkin to bed so we can talk properly."

Spencer nodded and sipped the wine while Jenna disappeared.

Oh, my days, thought Jenna, the second she entered the bedroom she shared with her sister and baby Zada. *What's he doing here and why do I have to be dressed in my flannelette pajamas that are about seven years old?*

She popped Zada in her crib and kissed her forehead. Zada was as good as gold. There were rarely tantrums at bedtime. She had a routine the family stuck rigidly to, which resulted in a well-mannered, easygoing child. Breathing in and out a few times, Jenna shrugged her shoulders to release the nervous tension.

Spencer looked heavenly in his sharp business suit. He hadn't shaved since their date and his stubble was turning into a beard, which seemed all the rage. It covered his pronounced jaw line and gave him an animalistic appeal with his broad shoulders and muscular arms. He was different to any other man she'd ever met. Turning round, she half expected him to be in the doorway looking her up and down like a piece of meat. Instead, he'd given her some privacy.

She strolled out to the kitchen and sat opposite him at the small square wooden dining table.

"I'm not sure whether I should change into something more appropriate for visitors or stay as I am."

"You look...." Spencer paused, "comfortable. Stay as you are. Unless, of course, you'd prefer to change," he said quickly, not wanting to sound dictatorial.

Jenna poured herself a wine. "Did you wind Ms. Princely round your finger so you could get that second date with me or was it out of a sense of duty?"

"Are your evenings free now?" quizzed Spencer.

"They are, my weekends as well. I have an earlier start, but I'm doing a bit of housekeeping and cleaning for an elderly lady who lives close to the campus. Same hours but it fits in better with my studies and makes life easier all around. It's ideal, if I'm honest."

"Good, I'm glad."

Jenna was disappointed. Her hazel eyes met Spencer's but she couldn't read what was going on in his mind.

"Would you still like that second date?" asked Spencer evenly.

It was such a formal invite. Jenna was now concerned he was asking her because he felt obligated, not because he wanted to.

"I guess."

"You guess? That doesn't sound too promising," teased Spencer. "I go crawling to Ms. Princely begging her to free your schedule up in order so that I have the opportunity to get to know you better and you aren't even certain you want a second date?"

"Maybe I don't want to seem too eager."

"Throwing yourself at me would be a bit college girl and quite the turn off," agreed Spencer.

Standing up, he walked to Jenna and offered her a hand. She took it and stood up. His fingers went to the buttons of her pajama top. Slowly, he began to unbutton it and let the thick pink material part.

"And I have very little interest in girls."

Jenna's chest was heaving as her flawless brown skin was revealed. She could feel Spencer's eyes devouring her breasts against the cream-colored bra. Having unbuttoned her as low as her navel he was able to push the dowdy pajama top over her shoulders and watch it fall to the ground. The college girl in her comfort clothes had disappeared. In front of Spencer stood a coffee colored goddess in a matching cream lacy underwear set.

His hands cupped her face and tilted her head towards his. His warm lips landed on her plush ruby ones. Without hesitation, Jenna let her lips part and felt Spencer's tongue press into her mouth. Standing nearly naked next to his fully clothed six-foot-two frame was weird. Jenna felt exposed and vulnerable, yet hugely sexy. With eyes shut, the kiss seemed to last forever. When Spencer did break the lip lock, he remained holding her face.

"Are you more than just a clever college girl able to hold her own with the adults, Jenna King?" The question was patronizing. She went to pull her head back, but Spencer's grip was firm. He kissed her affectionately. "I don't want to waste my time here."

"Neither do I and my mum and sister are due home in less than two hours." Her hazel eyes were blazing.

Honestly, he makes one phone call to my boss and suddenly he thinks he's earned the top spot in my list of priorities, she thought.

"I can see you're angry."

"Good," she snapped.

"Jenna, I want you to listen to me." Something in his voice resonated with her.

"We've wasted days. That's days I could've spent getting to know you. I don't want to waste any more time."

Her eyes softened as she remembered his niece.

"I'm not used to college girls. I'm not used to having to speak to employers to bail out my

girl—" He stopped before using the word girlfriend. "I'm not used to having to speak to employers to bail out potential lovers because of some clause or contract in what's nothing more than a part- time job. I'm certainly not used to high-rise buildings without working elevators and ex-boyfriends in jail."

"Any other part of my life you'd like to tear apart?"

133

"I'm not tearing apart your life. I'm trying to highlight the differences so you're aware of the obstacles in blending our lifestyles."

"That's a fair point," reasoned Jenna, "but you can't hold me accountable because I wasn't born with a silver spoon in my mouth."

"I'm not," he said. "And you shouldn't hold it against me because I was."

"It's difficult," sighed Jenna.

The weariness in her voice concerned Spencer. He'd gone to great lengths to express what trials they'd faced and he'd now possibly put her off even contemplating dating him. It was the last thing he wanted. "But not impossible," he asserted.

Releasing her face, he put a hand on her waist to turn her gently from him. Rotating Jenna slowly, he was able to pull her petite but curvaceous figure back into him. He lifted the straightened weave from her neck to enable his lips to brush the sensitive skin of her throat. His warm breath and feathery kisses brought up gooseflesh. There was something strong but sensitive in his touch and Jenna was unable to resist. His teeth went to her earlobe and the grazing of them had her damp between the legs. He sucked on her ear lobe.

His free hand, resting on her shoulder, traced the outside of her arm. Spencer could feel Jenna shivering. Running his fingers back up the inside of her arm, he let his palm slide down the length of her body. As his hand ran over the cup of her bra, Jenna's nipples hardened. He relished her soft skin, tiny waist and rounded hips. Pushing his pelvis forward slightly, Jenna was able to feel his hard-on.

Spencer stopped by the elastic of Jenna's panties. His thumb hooked over them and he moved his hand round. That one digit, frighteningly close to her pubic mound, made Jenna grind her behind against Spencer's erection. His breathing became more audible and ragged. Turning her neck slightly, Jenna's eyes were able to meet Spencer's, which were clouded with lust. His mouth went to hers to reassure her this wasn't merely about leaving her home sexually satisfied.

As the kiss deepened, Spencer's hand moved inside her panties. His middle finger located her clit and he pressed firmly on it. Jenna's body physically weakened at the sensation. He slid the finger down the crevice of her pussy to feel how wet she was. Pleased by the dripping, he let his finger slide up and down and around her clit. Jenna began grinding against him to increase the pressure; feeling electric tingles build inside her.

The second Jenna reacted dominantly to his touch, Spencer removed his hand. Her back to him, Jenna could hear him taste her as he sucked his finger. Without a word of direction, Spencer's hand went to Jenna's back to lower her face down to the dining room table. Jenna allowed herself to bend over and outstretched her arms to grip the table.

She could hear Spencer unbuckling his belt. The sound of his fly unzipping encouraged Jenna to part her legs slightly to permit him access to her needy pussy. Spencer's hand on the bare skin of her back, massaged her firmly as he released his cock. He shuffled closer, preparing to embed himself in her. In a quick movement, Jenna's panties were bunched aside. The material rubbing to one side of her thigh and Spencer's hand gripping her buttock was the ultimate foreplay. In seconds, she could feel his throbbing shaft slide between the lips of her pussy. Teasing her, he let his helmet rub over her clit as his rod taunted the entrance to her slit.

In an unexpectedly gracious movement, he thrust himself into Jenna's tight entrance. She gasped aloud at the width of him as he glided up inside her. She tightened her grip on the corners of the table. Spencer bucked his hips, letting his eight inches delve deeper and deeper inside the stunning woman in front of him. Finally finding his rhythm, rather than pound her for his own pleasure, Spencer's motion became smoother and longer.

He lowered slightly to bring his body closer to Jenna's. As he plunged in further he gyrated his hips, brushing the sensitive nerve endings inside Jenna. She spread her legs and rounded her ass to ensure she was able to accommodate the full length of him. Part of her felt strange being naked while Spencer was fully clothed, but another part of her enjoyed the element of danger that her mother or sister may arrive home earlier than anticipated. Spencer clearly had the same notion as he began to increase his pace.

A hand on her shoulder held her firmly in place as he jerked inside her, while he let his other hand creep around her thigh to find her bud again. It took him seconds to locate the slippery nub. He pinched it between his thumb and forefinger causing Jenna to whimper. Spencer continued to manipulate her clit, gauging Jenna's pleasure from the shaking of her legs.

She was soon begging him in a whisper to stop or take her to the brink. He let us forefinger and middle finger caress her clit in a constant movement until she was bucking on his cock and gritting her teeth to stop from screaming out. The sensation of her jerking and releasing on him had Spencer driving his shaft harder and faster into her.

Removing his hand from between her legs, his hands stretched out to cover hers. Holding her securely to the table, he was in a position to pound her relentlessly. Deliberately holding back from his own peak, Spencer was drilling Jenna to the point where her body was exhausted from his passion. As she reached a point where she was no longer able to keep up with his raw and rough taking of her, Spencer finally released his load inside her. His body collapsed on hers for a few seconds. Jenna could feel his heart pounding in his chest through his shirt.

"Sorry, sorry," he apologized, realizing his weight may be crushing her.

Jenna wasn't certain what the apology was for. The sex was rough, but not in a horrid way. She felt longed after and secure in his presence. She was disappointed to feel him peeling himself away and adjusting his attire.

With what remaining strength she had left, Jenna managed to force herself up from the table. Turning to face him, she stumbled slightly over her own feet. Spencer steadied her and lifted her to sit on the table. He spread her legs at the knees and moved between them.

"I could happily take you again," he smiled wolfishly, pulling at the strap of her bra.

"People have to eat off this table," she laughed.

"But they don't have to know what's happened on it."

She slapped his hands away from her bra straps. "Stop it!"

He kissed her shoulder and then her mouth. His heart felt light, but as his eyes adjusted to the room, he remembered where he was, and how the night would unfold.

"I suppose you should-"

"I need to make myself decent," countered Jenna, fully aware he was looking to make a quick getaway to avoid meeting her family.

"I don't mean it to sound like that. There's nothing I'd like more than to spend the night with you."

She could tell he wasn't paying her lip service.

"You have to admit, your living situation doesn't lend itself to that," he explained.

"No, but yours does."

He nodded.

"Will you at least wait for me to have a shower and change, or do you plan on dashing out in the night."

"I have no plans on leaving you stranded. I'm not that callous. I came to see you, to see if you wanted to see me. The idea wasn't to pop round, get my end away and walk out." Spencer's tongue tripped on the words.

"I won't be long."

Spencer watched as her toned, pert figure strode toward the bathroom. He resisted the urge to follow her in and watch.

Chapter Seven

Spencer yawned and stretched his arms over his head. The second he heard keys being rattled and inserted in various locks, he straightened up immediately and tried to look alert. A younger, plumper version of Jenna entered the house.

"Hello," she said cautiously. "If you're who I think you are, then I don't have to worry about you burgling the apartment and clearing out the family silver."

Spencer rolled his eyes. Jenna clearly had been confiding in her sister.

"You must be Zada's mother. Liana, is it?"

"That's right. You must be the British billionaire."

"Spencer Lawson," he offered by ways of introduction.

Liana studied the hand he'd extended. She could see his hair was damp and parts of his shirt were sweaty from exertion.

"No thanks, I don't know where that's been," said Liana smartly.

"Liana!" Jenna was standing in the kitchen dressed in jogging pants and a sleeveless top.

"Sorry," she apologized to Spencer.

Spencer had already withdrawn his hand, embarrassed by Jenna's sister's accurate observations.

"Guess you're heading out now," said Liana.

Spencer's eyes flickered over to Jenna. She threw him a sympathetic smile to let him know she bore no malice with him wanting to flee the scene of the crime with her outspoken sister now present.

"It's early. I'm in no hurry."

Liana's mouth dropped open in surprise in response.

Spencer flopped on the worn checkered couch. His massive frame took up most of it. Jenna could feel herself wanting to catch flies like her sister, but was impressed with Spencer's effort. Grabbing two cans of soda from the fridge, Jenna settled in next to him. He draped an arm around her shoulder and opened his soft drink.

Jenna switched on the TV and began channel hopping. She had no real clue what Spencer liked watching. He seemed more like a bookworm or art gallery lover than a guy who was happy to veg out on the couch watching TV. Finding a black and white film, Jenna hoped it was tasteful and cultured enough to entertain Spencer.

Spencer gave her a queer look. Jenna shrugged. He took the remote from her and continued flicking through the channels, until eventually settling on a repeat of a popular American comedy show.

"Are you two for real?" blurted out Liana.

They both looked over at her with quizzical expressions.

"Jenna, seriously, since when do you have a boyfriend stop over to watch repeats of 'Friends' while babysitting? And what's with a billionaire casually sitting in a cheap rented apartment drinking a home brand soda?"

"I wouldn't have thought as a single mom living at home, you could afford to be so judgmental," said Jenna cattily.

"Girls," growled Spencer in a low voice.

The sisters looked at one another. Were they being reprimanded in their own house?

"Baby Zada's asleep," reminded Spencer. "Liana, how was college tonight?"

"Fine," she answered without thinking. "Stressful, actually. I have some big assignments coming up and I'm pushed for time."

"Have you eaten?"

"Not yet."

"Neither have I," said Spencer. "I've worked up quite the appetite. Should I order in for us?"

This really is too bizarre, thought Jenna. *He's gone*

from Mr. Cool to big brother in minutes.

"I'm not sure they do take out sushi," said Liana slyly, sitting on a single sofa chair.

"Actually they do, but it's not very filling," Spencer informed her amiably. "I was thinking more along the lines of pizza."

"That would be kind of great." Liana's voice was warmer.

"You two decide what you want and order. I'm just going to use the bathroom." Spencer went out to the bathroom. He washed his hands and splashed cold water on his face.

"This could be a nightmare if you let it be," he told himself as he stared in the mirror. "But instead of faking enthusiasm, see where it goes. Liana's bright and she's got a tongue on her. She cares about her sister and so do you. That's something you have in common."

In terms of his relationship with Jenna, they weren't exactly at the stage where he should be meeting her family. In fact, he was nowhere close to it and he personally didn't think he was in the wrong feeling uncomfortable with the situation. That said, the last time he'd made love to Jenna, he'd inadvertently put his foot in things by asking if she planned on leaving his bed before or after she'd done his cleaning. It wasn't enough to make a grand gesture by arriving at her home and asking her on a second date. He owed it

143

to her to make sure she didn't feel used by him again.

He stepped out of the bathroom to see Liana on the phone reeling off an order. Walking slowly over, he took his place on the couch. Truthfully, he couldn't remember the last time he'd spent an evening in watching TV. Mostly he split his time between work and going out. There was something quite pleasant about the warmth of Jenna snuggled up next to him.

Liana went to check on Zada.

"Why a black and white film?" he asked Jenna incredulously.

"Because it's cultured and arty and I thought you were cultured and arty."

"Do you know when that film was made?"

"The thirties?"

"Talkies were around then, but that film was made in 2011. It's French and it won a lot of Oscars. I've already seen it."

"I was right, though," she said smugly.

"How?"

"It's foreign and cultured and arty and you've seen it. Therein, my assumption that you're cultured and arty is correct."

"Wrong. I saw it because I attended the premiere. I

don't habitually watch black and white movies. They're way before my time. I'm the kind of guy that likes to keep things current, hence my involvement with technology."

"Oh." Jenna was quiet. She felt foolish. Spencer probably attended loads of premieres. That was the point he'd made earlier. Their life experiences were vastly different and it was clearly going to affect their relationship.

"Don't look down," he said softly. "The whole point of us spending time together is to allow us to get to know one another. Now you know I like movie premieres but keep up with current trends."

"And what do you know about me?"

"That you're very quick in the shower and that you and sister can easily be at loggerheads with one another."

"Sorry about Liana."

"Don't apologize on behalf of your sister. She didn't say anything untrue. She's upfront and she clearly cares about you."

A sharp rap at the door had Liana sprinting out of her bedroom toward the front door. As Liana carted in an array of pizza boxes and ice cream, Spencer went to settle up the bill.

"Thanks, Spencer," said Liana between mouthfuls of

stuffed crust pizza. "I'm famished. This will give me the energy I need to get on with my assignments."

"Li, you're eating like you haven't been fed in a month," chastised Jenna.

"Don't be precious. It smells heavenly and it tastes heavenly."

"You aren't eating for two anymore."

Spencer smiled inwardly. He could see why Liana was carrying a few extra pounds on her sister, but the comment was harsh. Liana's face was thunderous; her sister's triumphant.

"Liana, about your coursework," interjected Spencer before World War 3 broke out.

"Mmmhmmm."

"Perhaps I could help you out a little and free up some time for you to invest in your studies."

Jenna looked at him admiringly. He certainly was getting hands-on with involving himself in her family affairs.

"What were you thinking?" asked Liana.

"I have contacts with some personal nannies over here. If it helps at all, I'm using their services next week and would be happy to place Zada with my regular one."

"Uh uh, no way," answered Liana.

"Geez, Li. Can you think about how you sound?" frowned Jenna.

"What? I'm not having my baby placed with a stranger."

"Of course," agreed Spencer hoping to calm things. "It was a foolish suggestion."

"It wasn't a foolish suggestion," countered Jenna putting a hand on his arm.

"I should make a move."

"Spencer, no," urged Jenna.

"I completely forgot I have my driver waiting downstairs. I shouldn't leave him for hours on end."

"Wow, you've been up here enjoying my sister's...company...and stuffing your face while some poor sap's minding your car. What a life."

Spencer bit his tongue to refrain from saying that he and Jenna had barely had a chance to taste the pizza with Liana's ravenous appetite.

"I'll leave you two to it."

"Let me walk you out," insisted Jenna.

"No," said Spencer, his voice verging on curt. "Stay in, where it's safe and enjoy your dinner."

"Will we speak later?" Jenna could hear her voice bleating. Spencer nodded and waited for Jenna to unbolt the door.

"Thanks for dinner Spencer," shouted Liana.

"No problem."

Spencer kissed Jenna's forehead and walked out.

"What were you thinking behaving like that," shouted Jenna at her sister after she shut the door.

"What?"

"How could you be so rude?"

"I'm not leaving my baby with a stranger."

"Spencer clearly has a relationship with the nanny service. If he trusts them, then they aren't strangers."

"They're strangers to me and you and they'd be a stranger to Zada."

"They'd provide excellent care and you'd have had a way to continue your studies in assignment week without interruption," argued Jenna.

"The best care for my daughter is from family."

"And what if Spencer becomes family one day?"

"Listen to yourself, Jenna. You've had one date with the guy and now you're marrying him? Get over the fairytale complex. It's not going to last. You're a novelty for him. He wants a taste of what it's like to rough it."

Liana's comments stung. It was what Jenna feared about dating Spencer. It was one thing her thinking it, but if her sister was as well, did that mean everyone doubted Spencer's intentions? Tears pricked her eyes. She didn't want Liana to know she'd delivered a blow to her confidence.

"If he wanted to taste common, he'd have chosen to date you and not me."

Liana jumped up. "What's that supposed to mean?"

"Look at yourself, Li. You come in and make vulgar comments to someone upon your first meeting with them. The second he offers to buy dinner, you go to town and over-order. Then when he tries to constructively offer help, you treat him like dirt. You hardly came across as the picture of civility."

"At least I'm not trying to be someone I'm not."

"I would never treat another human being the way you did."

"Not when he's got billions in his bank account," said Liana snidely.

"I wouldn't care if he had cents in his account. He didn't deserve that."

"He's trying to worm his way in, Jen. We're a case

study for him; a family for him to play philanthropist to while increasing his public profile. You're totally deluded if you think otherwise."

"You're totally deluded if you think I'm going to spend my nights in babysitting and missing out on time with Spencer so you can attend night classes."

"Well I'm glad you know where your loyalties lie," hissed Liana.

"Family loyalty means you support one another's dreams - not destroy them. I'll be surprised if Spencer ever wants to talk to me again."

*

Jenna was mortified by her sister's behavior. She rang Spencer to apologize but his phone went straight through to voicemail. She sent a text but that too went unanswered.

Spencer stared up at the intricate plasterwork of his white bedroom ceiling. Jenna wasn't responsible for her sister's attitude. Punishing her wasn't fair, but at the same time the interaction highlighted that Spencer was out of touch with the 'common people' and socially didn't blend well in a family environment. Yet, he seemed to have had a normal upbringing and considered his own family to be tight knit.

Perhaps brotherhood was easier than having mixed siblings. Spencer had a close bond with both his brothers. They certainly hadn't clashed the way

Jenna and Liana did. At first he'd found the sibling rivalry amusing, but it hadn't taken long for it to turn to discomfort. He was only glad Jenna's mother hadn't been present.

Too much estrogen and not enough testosterone, he thought glibly. *This would be a lot easier to walk away from if I hadn't enjoyed Jenna's company.*

He had and because of that, he wasn't prepared to close the door on the relationship quite yet. Being unfamiliar with the situation made it difficult for him to decide what his next move should be. He needed to get out of bed and prepare for the gym before the cleaner arrived, but he was finding it hard to muster the incentive. The idea of Mrs. Kozak arriving and finding him lounging naked in his bed was not a pleasant scenario. Dragging himself out of bed, he flung on his gym attire, thankful his apartment building had its own gym.

Opening his front door, he was surprised to see Jenna there.

"Are you back to clean my apartment?" he asked cheekily.

Jenna put a hand to his face. She'd expected coolness or anger, not gentle teasing. His understanding touched her.

"Forgive me?"

"You didn't do anything wrong, Jenna."

"No, but I shouldn't have put you in that position."

"You didn't, I did." he said firmly, implying that no woman ran or controlled his schedule. "You actually gave me the go ahead to leave, if memory serves correctly."

"Bet you wished you'd taken me up on the offer and not tried to be so gallant."

Mrs. Kozak appeared. Head down, she nodded politely.

"God I hope she doesn't report that to Ms. Princely," muttered Jenna.

"She won't and even if she did, there's nothing that can be done now. The whole purpose of moving you from my apartment was so that we could see each other again."

"Until my sister opened her stupid mouth, preventing you from ever wanting to see me again."

Spencer began heading to the elevator. Jenna picked up her pace to keep up with him. "Jenna, do you actually think I'm so weak-willed that your sister's behavior would affect my feelings for you?"

"Not exactly. I think her rudeness last night makes me an unattractive prospect."

"Trust me, there is nothing unattractive about you," said Spencer, punching the basement button.

"Where do we go from here then?"

Spencer studied her. Jenna was forthright like her sister but there was a warmth and sincerity to her. He admired her boldness. Not a lot of women would risk rejection by initiating a conversation in regard to the second date.

"You aren't babysitting Saturday night?"

"No," replied Jenna quickly.

"We'll do something Saturday then."

"As in tomorrow?"

"Sure."

"Are you going to tell me what we'll be doing?"

Jenna pressed the ground floor button to let herself out, sensing the conversation had reached a natural end.

"I haven't decided yet."

"You're being very mysterious."

"I thought women liked surprises."

"Yes, but given recent events I'd like to ensure I have the correct wardrobe for any surprises."

"I'll call you," he promised as the door to the lift opened.

Jenna kissed him firmly on the mouth.

"Make sure you do."

It wasn't until he was running on the treadmill that Spencer was able to clear his head. Next week was going to be busy. His niece would be over to see a specialist regarding her condition. What he didn't want was anything interfering with that aspect of his life. His love life was still of tabloid interest. Doing something public with Jenna could generate unwanted publicity. It'd be best to play things down for the moment. That didn't mean he couldn't treat Jenna to something special – it just couldn't be local.

The big question was what to do tonight. It'd been a week ago that he'd taken Jenna as his date to the charity gala dinner. Since then, his nights had been spent in the apartment as he'd attempted to mend his mistakes with Jenna and rectify her working situation. He couldn't recall the last time he'd spent six nights keeping a low profile. After last night's blow up, he wanted to let off some steam and be by himself and free of the trials and tribulations that appeared to come with dating Jenna King.

On no account was he intending to return to Jenna's apartment in the near future after Liana's tepid welcome. As she was due to babysit, it made sense that Spencer do his own thing. It wasn't as if he were chained to Jenna or obligated to spend his every free moments with her.

***

Jenna spent her Friday night indoors taking care of Zada and packing an overnight case. Spencer had called during the day telling her that he'd be sending a car for her at 6 am Saturday morning and to wear something comfortable and to expect to stay overnight. It sounded casual enough, and given he'd bought her outfit to the charity gala dinner he clearly knew the limitations of her wardrobe. If he genuinely wanted to get to know her better, maybe the plan was to spend the weekend cozied up in his apartment. It might be intimate and give them time together, but she couldn't help feeling a little disappointed that he wasn't taking her out on the town. The charity gala dinner had been fun and Jenna had proved she could work the scene with ease. She'd been hoping for something similar on their second date.

When the car arrived for Jenna early Saturday morning, she was surprised to see a sleepy looking Spencer in the back seat, waiting for her with a lazy kiss.

"You look as though you haven't been to bed," she remarked.

His lip curling in a smile suggested he hadn't. Jenna wasn't sure whether she liked the idea of him being out all night. If he had been – where had he been and with whom?

"Champagne?" offered Spencer grandly.

"Spencer, it's just past 6 am. Isn't it a bit early?"

"It's midday where we're headed. I'd say it's exactly the right time to start the celebrations."

"What do you mean where we're headed?"

Jenna realized they were on the way to JFK airport. The car followed a private route that took them directly onto a secluded part of the tarmac.

"Paris. Dinner tonight."

"But I haven't bought anything to wear," screeched Jenna.

"Don't worry. There'll be time to shop when we arrive."

Jenna knocked back the champagne. She was heady with excitement. The chartered plane was slick and sleek. The pilot and a pretty flight attendant greeted them. Jenna noted Spencer's surname "Lawson" on the tail of the plane and guessed he owned the private aircraft.

"There's a tail wind so we'll make good time," said the pilot over the intercom.

"I can't believe I was disappointed by your lack of imagination," said a shamefaced Jenna.

"What? Did you think I was going to lock you in my apartment for the weekend and make you watch black and white movies?" mocked a somewhat more animated Spencer.

"Something like that."

"I'm glad I'm not overly predictable. I suspect most women would think I am."

"Well, I'm not like most women."

"Time will tell," said Spencer cynically.

Spencer's cynicism disappeared over the course of the weekend. Without the pressure of work or family, the twosome were able to relax. Spencer enjoyed seeing old things through new eyes. Having a helicopter on the tarmac of Charles De Gaulle airport to fly him to the helipad of the Hotel Georg V was standard practice for Spencer. Jenna, however, had never travelled in a helicopter before, let alone stayed at a hotel where a helicopter could land. Bought up with permanently stretching household finances meant that this was Jenna's first trip out of the United States.

Visiting Macy's for a makeover to attend the charity gala dinner had been one thing, but shopping at the exclusive Gallerias Lafayette department store was something else altogether. Jenna felt out of her depth, wandering through the women's fashion department, but with Spencer by her side, she was treated like royalty.

Now I really do feel like I'm in a romantic movie, she thought.

She couldn't have been any more in awe of the

Parisian vibe than being treated to a six course meal at the Le Jules Verne restaurant nested in the Eiffel Tower itself. The food was exquisite, as were the views.

Upon entering the Royal Suite to prepare for bed, Jenna was in a marble bathroom with sauna and steam room. Crystal chandeliers lit the room that was perfumed by vases of pale pink roses and decorated with French antiques. The four-poster sumptuous bed was as divine as Spencer's lovemaking.

Breakfast in bed after a night of passion and endless chatter was the perfect end to their brief visit to Paris. Landing back in JFK, it was as if the weekend were a dream concocted by Jenna's vividly romantic notions.

"Will I see you this week?" asked Jenna, aware of Spencer's commitment to his niece during her stay.

"We'll sort something out."

He kissed her gently, feeling something like a cross between deep caring and huge likability in his heart for the innocent, but realistic social worker-to-be.

"Would you like me to walk you inside?" asked Spencer, nodding up to Jenna's front door.

"Spencer, you've done more than enough for me for one weekend. I don't really think I can ask you to face Liana right now. She has a habit of spoiling your kindest gestures."

He kissed her tenderly. "You're worth facing her wrath for."

"All the same, I'll let you off tonight."

"I won't pretend I'm not grateful," grinned Spencer.

They kissed again and Jenna skipped out of the car with a load of shopping bags as well as the tiny overnight bag she'd bought.

She opened the main reception door. Sitting on the steps patiently was her ex-boyfriend Leon.

"Hey Jenna, guess who got let out early for good behavior?"

Chapter Eight

Jenna dropped all her shopping bags at the sight of her ex-boyfriend. She wasn't threatened by Leon, she'd grown up with him and he'd always been good to her, but seeing him on the stairs was a shock given he'd been in jail for well over a year.

"Didn't mean to scare you," he said apologetically. "I was looking forward to seeing you."

She couldn't even reprimand Leon for stalking her because he lived in the same building as her.

"When'd you get out?" she uttered.

"Saturday."

She couldn't think of anything to say.

"I did say the other week when you were visiting, I was looking at getting an early release."

Her eyes were wide as she tried to take in the boy she'd grown up with sitting in front of her. Except he wasn't a boy now. Leon was all man. He was big and broad and had the build of a heavyweight boxer.

"I wasn't expecting it to be that quick."

"I thought it'd be a surprise for you," he said softly.

"Well it is that," she chuckled.

They'd made an agreement when Leon landed in jail, that they'd keep their distance from one another. Leon would let Jenna get on with her life so that she could turn things around and get a degree and help other teens like them from a deprived background. Leon had assured her he'd use his time in prison wisely to educate himself in order that he could leave gang life.

There had never been any discussions of reuniting. Even when she'd been asked to visit him recently, because Spencer had been investigating her background, he'd been adamant he'd stay out of her way after release, so as not to interfere with her progress. Now, here he was, waiting on the steps as if they were both fifteen again.

"Can an old friend ask for a hug?"

It seemed mean saying no, but at the same time, Jenna knew she could be sending out the wrong signal by agreeing to it. His big brown eyes were akin to an excited puppy and she felt her heart melt.

"Course."

She hugged him lightly and noticed his grip on her was tight, like that of a man being thrown a life ring cushion while drowning at sea. Jenna had released her embrace some time before Leon finally let go of her.

"You look good," he commented with his big white innocent smile (which was anything but innocent).

She shut her eyes. It was too easy to go back there and it wasn't fair of Leon to do this to her – not after the weekend she'd just had.

"Thanks." Jenna opted not to return to the compliment. The situation was awkward and she didn't know how to extricate herself from it. She began collecting her shopping bags.

"You want a hand with those?"

Again, it seemed churlish to refuse. "Leon, Mom's in and you know how she feels about you. I can do without the argument tonight. It's probably best I manage them alone."

"Yeah, of course," he said quietly.

She could feel him watching her as she arranged the bags in a way that she'd be able to manage the stairs.

"Elevator's still broken?"

"Some things never change, Leon."

"Bad luck for me on floor fifteen."

Jenna grimaced on his behalf. That was a lot of stairs to trek. "How does your mom manage?" The words were out of her mouth before she could stop them. She'd made a rookie error by showing an interest. He'd translate an interest in his mom as an interest in him.

"Elevator around the other end of the building works

fine. It's a longer walk, but preferable to the stairs."

The conversation was sounding hollow and forced. Jenna wondered if Leon felt the same. He reached out and tugged one of Jenna's bags.

"That French?"

She noticed he was pointing to the writing on the shopping bag's logo.

"Yeah. Don't tell me you were studying another language while you were banged up?"

He laughed and the sound was rich and real. "No. I just knew it wasn't English. Lucky guess."

They remained staring at each other. Jenna couldn't get up the stairs until he moved and Leon didn't look as if he were in any rush.

"There are French shops round here or something? Because that would be a change."

"No," she huffed impatiently.

"Where'd you get it then?"

"Leon, please. I need to get upstairs."

"Sure, of course. I was looking forward to seeing you. I kept an eye out for you all weekend and it's only now I've found you."

"I was away, Leon."

"In France?" he teased.

"Yes." The bold statement rung around the staircase.

"Seriously?"

"Yes," said Jenna more quietly.

"Well good on you girl."

Leon stood up.

What hurt Jenna most was that he sounded as though he meant it. He sounded as though he was pleased she'd been lucky enough to score a weekend in Paris. There was no bitter resentment there. Jenna felt sick to the pit of her stomach.

"I need to go."

"Jenna--Jen!"

She raced up the stairs and prayed Leon wouldn't follow her. Keys in various locks, she let herself in, threw her bags on the ground and raced to the toilet where she proceeded to vomit.

"Baby girl, are you okay?" It was her mother's concerned voice.

"I'm fine," she shouted.

As she retched until there was nothing left in her stomach, Jenna finally collapsed on the floor. She rested her head on the cool porcelain of the sink. *Of*

all the times for Leon to re-enter her life, why now?
Closing her eyes and taking some deep breaths, she
gathered her strength. Running the cold water tap she
stood to wash her face and brush her teeth. She tried
opening the bathroom door quietly but her mother
was standing there - arms crossed and waiting for an
explanation.

"I told you he'd find her." Liana's voice sailed
through the apartment.

"Shut up Liana," chanted Jenna and her mother.

Liana walked over. "You know he's back then?" she
asked kindly, putting a blanket round her sister's
shoulders.

"Yes."

"He promised to stay away," muttered Jenna's
mother.

"When did he ever keep a promise?" grumbled Liana
stonily.

"How'd you know he was back?" Jenna asked her
sister.

"He's been loitering round the staircase all weekend.
I didn't tell him where you'd been or who you were
with. I didn't even say you'd gone away. I said if you
wanted to be found, you would be."

Ultimately, despite their differences, the two sisters
would do anything for one another.

"And you spoke to him?" asked Hannah, her mother.

Jenna looked at her mother. Even before she answered, she could see the disapproval in her mother's eyes.

"I couldn't just ignore him." Was her answer.

"Of course you could. You didn't have to say a word. Now see the state you're in."

"Mom. We've known Leon forever. What was Jenna supposed to do?" interjected Liana.

"Tell him to mind his own business."

"It's not that easy," argued Jenna. "I think he's turned himself around."

"And how would you know that? He hasn't even been out for forty-eight hours. Already he's working his silver tongue on you."

"The fact that he didn't serve his full sentence speaks volumes."

Liana rolled her eyes at her sister. Defending Leon wasn't going to calm their mother down.

"It says he knows how to work the system."

"Stop being cynical, mom. I changed, why can't Leon?"

Her mother was furious and Jenna had to share a bed

with her.

What a rotten end to the weekend, she thought.

"Keep your head on your shoulders," warned her mother. "I'm not around to force Leon to keep away from you. He's a bad influence. That's why you ended up involved in silly, stupid, dangerous games as a teenager. I blamed myself because I work three jobs but what could I do. Nothing's changed. I still work three jobs to support us and I can't take time off to protect you. I only hope you've grown up and have the sense to stay away from whatever he cooks up. You've got a new life and a future. Focus on that. Focus on this billionaire; he'll give you more than Leon ever could."

Jenna was on the verge of having a rip-roaring row with her mother. They hadn't fought in ages. Not since Leon was sentenced. One ten-minute conversation regarding her ex and they were already circling each other like wild cats ready to pounce.

"Money doesn't maketh the man, mother."

Liana could see the two women were reaching boiling point.

"Jenna, come in my bedroom. I want to hear about Paris and I'm desperate to see what's in all those bags you've bought back. There's nothing we can do about Leon now. Don't let him ruin Jenna's weekend mom, not when it was her first time out of the country."

Hannah relented. She didn't trust Leon and she never would. She only hoped Jenna had the good sense to remember a leopard never changed its spots.

*

Spencer made an executive decision to allow Jenna twenty-four hours to recover from their rushed weekend in Paris. Jenna still had her studies and was still contracted to Ms. Princely at Supreme Cleaning Services, so had obligations to fulfill. Spencer's insistence that she be at his beck and call, allowing him to finance their relationship, was not one that instilled a feeling of security or equality in their burgeoning romance. He knew better to even put the suggestion to Jenna.

Having collected his parents, brother and niece from JFK Airport, he arranged for the family to be driven to the luxurious town house on Fifth Avenue that Spencer purchased for his parents some years back. Spencer had the house cleaned, stocked and prepared for the guests. He sat easily on the steps awaiting their arrival.

Greeting his petite mother bodily, and his sister-in-law with a kiss on the cheek, a firm handshake for his father and a brusque hug for his brother, Spencer bolted to the car seat to extract Rosie from the vehicle.

'Hey Rosie," he cooed softly. "Do you remember your Uncle Spencer?"

The pretty blonde haired, brown-eyed girl dressed

like a fancy china doll, said nothing. She wrung her hands and remained placid as Spencer carried her upstairs. Setting her straight in the cot, he sat cross-legged on the outside as if entranced by his niece. He passed her a soft toy with sensory materials attached for Rosie to look, feel and touch. She made no attempt to take the toy or play with it.

"It's okay, mate," said Spencer's brother, Rupert. "She can go in out of these little trances. It's been a long trip. She'll be more active when she'd less tired."

"Sure. I know I should know that," he said rubbing his eyes.

"Are you okay, Spencer, love?" asked his mother. "You look a little stressed."

"I probably am. Feel like I'm juggling a lot at the moment."

"You know we'll stay out of your way," said his father pleasantly. "It's not like we need to interfere in your life."

"Don't be proud, Dad. You're not interfering in my life. It's nice to have you here. Most of my friends still reside mainly in England. I only ever see them in New York when they're passing through. I enjoy the company of friends and family to the acquaintances I've made here."

"Is work bothering you, then?" probed his mother.

"No, no. Seriously don't worry about it."

The four standing adults exchanged a look.

Spencer was unable to see it because he was peering into Rosie's cot.

"It's a girl," mouthed Rosie's mother, Eloise.

There was snickering and Spencer's head popped up.

"Nothing old boy," assured Rupert. "Look, why don't you and I and dad go for a drink? There must be pubs around here."

"Bars more likely, but I'm sure we can find something suitable," agreed Spencer. With three females in this house, he suddenly felt very out of his depths.

"Not a dreadful sports bar," announced Mr. Lawson as they stood outside on the doorstep.

"No, Dad."

"And not a gentleman's club . The last thing I need is Eloise breathing down my neck and asking me five hundred questions."

"Rupert, I'm not sure I like what you're implying about my character, but I have no wish to spend an extortionate amount on strippers in the middle of the day with my brother and father present. All I want to do is spend time with my niece and ensure that her care and development is still top notch."

"I know old chap, we all want that," started Rupert, "but it's not a crime to think of yourself or outside of Rosie's Rett Syndrome. Don't let her or our family be defined by the blasted thing."

Rupert's hand on his shoulder calmed Spencer considerably. He flagged a yellow taxi to take them to The Churchill Tavern just off Madison Avenue. The pub was to the liking of all three men. Its decor was exceedingly British. The pub was dimly lit and even darker thanks to the brick walls and an old wooden bar and stools. Pleasing to the men's thirst and appetite, the premise's offered local British fare and craft beers.

The men opted for a booth and a pint of stout. One sip of the strong dark brew beer had Spencer wincing.

"Spending too much money on champagne?" laughed his father. "Forgotten your roots?"

"Not at all. I have beer in the fridge at home; this is just a particularly strong brew. It's a while since I've had something decent from a barrel."

Spencer listened to his father and brother talk shop. His brother was now a specialist in Rett Syndrome, making the professional change and undertaking the relevant studies and placements shortly after Rosie's diagnosis. His father remained a top neural surgeon, but as a doting granddad, had a strong interest in Rupert's niche area of medicine.

"You looked bored, Spence," remarked Rupert.

"No, just intimidated by all the medical jargon. When I hear you speak, I realize how actively you work toward helping Rosie. I feel I've the intention but unable to deliver anything useful."

"Spence, the charity gala dinner you held the other week brought in loads of money for the research department. You pay for all of Rosie's care and ensured we have a residence suitable for Rosie when she's growing up. Eloise and I could've afforded that, but we'd have spent a good part of our professional lives working to pay it off. That kind of work would've meant not spending precious time with our little girl.

The gifts you've given us extend beyond the materialistic. I can't put a price on what it's like not have to work long hours to support the extremely difficult living situation we have in catering to Rosie's syndrome. Your money helps, mate. It helps us to enjoy our little girl while we can. I hope my work helps but there's no guarantee on that. We see an instant response to your contribution to the family and the quality of Rosie's life."

Spencer smiled, but it was watery. He didn't feel useless, but it didn't abate his frustration about potentially never being able to communicate with his niece.

"Son," said Mr. Lawson, "Your devotion to the family is admirable and it comes naturally to you. You're thirty-two now. Do you ever think of settling down? Maybe stop playing the field and looking for someone who's better suited to you for more than just one night."

Only drunk in a pub could three British men have a realistic heart-to-heart.

"I need another drink."

"It wasn't until they were four pints along that Spencer was able to reveal his conundrum. "I have thought about settling down. No, not settling down so much as dating. Proper dating. The kind of dating with an end view of developing a relationship." His brown eyes were glassy, his face flushed, his body relaxed and his persona pleasant, thanks to his gentle inebriation.

"And who's the lucky lady to catch my brother's eye?"

"I'm not sure she thinks she's lucky."

"What woman landing a handsome billionaire born from my genetic pool wouldn't be a lucky lady?" guffawed Mr. Lawson.

"She's not a lady for a start."

His brother and father raised an amused eyebrow.

"She's not gentry," carried on Spencer.

"Spencer, we aren't in the Victorian era," guffawed his father.

"Yes, I know that, father. I mean she's from a very different background to ours."

"So the lady is a tramp," giggled Rupert.

Spencer's hand slammed on the table so hard all three glasses spilt.

"NO!"

"Calm down, mate. I was joking."

"She's not a tramp. In the right clothes and in the right place she's a complete lady. It's only her background doesn't afford the right clothes or opportunities to enter my playground."

Silence stretched between the family. Rupert wasn't trying to flare Spencer's temper, nor offend his love interest. He was being cryptic about the girl, which meant he clearly had some reservations.

"I've always thought a lady wasn't born with the title, nor could it be bred into her. A lady is defined by how she conducts herself in the company of other's and how she chooses to spend her time," mused Mr. Lawson.

If that definition is anything to go by, then Jenna totally fits the bill of being a lady, thought Spencer.

"Let's drop it," said Spencer. "It's all very complicated and I'm starting to see double, so I don't think you'll get much sense out of me for too much longer.

The men ordered another round of brown ale and returned to discussing football.

Chapter Nine

Jenna made her way into the diner after she finished her first set of classes on Tuesday morning. Her friend Kelly caught her eye and pointed to the section of the restaurant she was looking after.

"Is there going to be a stampede of college kids in two minutes," asked Kelly, stopping by Jenna's table.

"Maybe."

"You going to order?"

"You going to sit with me?" enquired Jenna.

"I can for a bit but let me take your order."

"Coffee."

"Jenna, work with me here. I can't just pour you endless bottomless cup of coffee and then sit and sympathize with you over the bad news."

"You've heard the news as well?"

"I didn't hear it so much as see it," said Kelly sympathetically.

Jenna contorted her face into an ugly expression of confusion.

"Have *you* actually seen it," asked Kelly tentatively.

Jenna shook her head.

"I'll get you pie with that coffee. Some hot apple pie to sweeten the sourness these pictures will leave in your mouth."

When Kelly returned, Jenna was grateful there hadn't been a stampede of customers creating a barrier between her and her friends.

"What'd you come to discuss then?" Kelly was trying to keep her voice airy.

"What pictures have you got?" fired back Jenna.

"They're not my pictures per se," evaded Kelly.

"Whom do they belong to?"

"A magazine."

Jenna snatched the magazine. Kelly made a poor attempt to stop her.

"Jen, I'm sorry. I thought you knew but if you didn't, then you deserve to."

Jenna flipped through the cheap rag full of glossy pictures and gossip. When she came to a section called 'Who's About Town' one of the first photos her eyes were draw to under the section 'Friday Night in NYC' was of Spencer.

Spencer was dressed in the exact same clothes he'd met her in early Saturday morning. And, he was adorned with a blonde on one arm, a brunette on the other and a gorgeous auburn haired oriental girl with her hand in his coat pocket following from behind as they exited the expensive Pacha club in Chelsea. Jenna thought she might be sick on the spot. She was relieved she hadn't touched the coffee or pie because it meant there was nothing in her stomach that could make her vomit.

"You didn't know?"

"Of course I didn't know. While he was arranging a private orgy, I was mistakenly packing for a romantic monogamous weekend away in Paris," spat Jenna bitterly.

"Did you go?"

"Of course I did. The magazine only came out..."Jenna's eyes scanned the inside front cover. "Last night."

"So you came here to tell me about your romantic getaway and I just dumped all over it by exposing that magazine to you."

"In fairness Kelly, the weekend was ruined when I left the limousine."

"Limousine? Words I bet you never imagined you'd be throwing into casual conversation." teased Kelly.

"After what you've just shown me, in all probability, it was my last ride."

"Jenna?" Kelly said more seriously, "Don't jump to conclusions. This guy has gone out of his way for you. I know as a couple you'll both have a natural set of problems to overcome because well let's face it, you're poor and he's rich, but don't make them more cumbersome by jumping to conclusions and causing a rift when you don't know what's happened.

It doesn't look good, but there could be a perfectly normal explanation to it. If you keep pushing him away, eventually he might take the hint and run and I know deep down, that's not what you want. It's not a healthy defense mechanism. Stop thinking you don't deserve to be in a healthy relationship with a nice man."

"It's not a healthy relationship if he doesn't want to spend his free time with me. I don't want to see him partying with other women, either. Why couldn't he take me out on Friday night?"

"Because you were packing."

"Well, he clearly got his packing done early in order that he could go out and withheld telling me about his plans to prevent me from joining him at Pacha."

"It does look a bit like that," agreed Kelly. She pulled her blonde hair out of its bun and gave it a shake.

"Hey Kelly, Health and safety, remember!" shouted her boss from behind the counter.

She narrowed her stormy blue eyes at him and began

putting her hair up again. "You going to tell me about Mr. British Billionaire and Paris then?"

"No," responded Jenna sternly.

"Why not? Don't be a spoil sport. That picture may mean nothing and it doesn't take away from what he did or how he was with you while you were in Paris.

"I didn't come here to talk to you about Paris, Kelly. I came to talk to you about something else."

"That being?"

"Leon."

"As in-"

"As in Leon my ex-boyfriend and now ex-con living in the same apartment building as us."

"Have you seen him?"

"Yes. I have this lovely romantic weekend with Spencer. I arrive back at our crummy building full of romance and memories and there's my childhood sweetheart, gazing up at me as if I'm the only woman on earth."

"Did you spit in his eye?"

"Don't be vulgar."

"I'm joking."

"Did you ignore him?"

"I couldn't. We have a history. I can't erase that or cut myself off from it. I was polite and civil and tried to remain at arm's length."

"Did you kiss him?"

"NOOOOOOOOO!"

"Did you want to?

"No," said Jenna in a whisper.

"Did you want him to kiss you?"

Jenna didn't answer.

"Your silence speaks volumes."

"He looks and acts as though he's grown up. The way he spoke and his consideration toward me. He was acting like how I was always telling him I wanted to be."

"How'd you leave things?"

"Vague. I can't encourage this, can I?"

"No!"

"You guys made a promise to each other that with all the love and good intentions in the world you're poison to one another and the most loving thing to do was free each other."

"We certainly were poison for each other when we made that vow."

"How long's he been out for?"

"It's his fourth day," confirmed Jenna.

"Someone's been counting."

"I'm always counting. Leon's been out of prison four days; Spencer hasn't called me in 36 hours."

"What are you going to do?"

"Well if Spencer's genuinely interested in me, he'll get in touch. I'm not going to chase him. He's probably resting his feet. I'm surprised the soles of his shoes weren't worn out chasing those three girls around on Friday night."

Kelly laughed. "Even so, he endured the pain of threadbare sneakers to get you to Paris. He's demonstrating something in there for you by not calling the weekend off after a hangover. You can't fault his commitment."

Jenna smiled. Rarely did she like people seeing her true feelings, particularly when it came to matters of the heart. Her love life with Leon had been a car crash that everyone witnessed. She couldn't bear the thought of going through the same thing again with Spencer so publicly.

"I wouldn't be surprised if I was part of some contest or joke he's devised with his posh pals."

182

"My God you're being paranoid and negative."

"What did you expect after those pictures?"

"I expected you to pick up the phone and ring him there and then for an explanation. I thought he liked your openness."

"Well I don't like how distant he is. If I stretch a hand out with an olive branch, I don't want to be humiliated when he slaps it away and reminds of the expiration dates of his lovers."

"I know that's not you talking," said Kelly, "but if you aren't in the mood, then I'll leave you to it and get on with things."

"What about Leon?" called Jenna as Kelly rose and wolfed down Jenna's pie for her.

"What about him? You're clearly more upset about Spencer Lawson than Leon, so deal with that first. Leon isn't someone you should be dealing with at all. If you're sensible you'll not invest any energy in that boy."

Jenna threw a note down to cover the charge and tip for Jenna. Her ears hated the advice but she respected Kelly for being a good friend and telling her how it was and directing her to the path that would bring the most happiness and the least risk. But Jenna wasn't always great at taking on board other people's advice. She had it in her head she could make everyone's lives better in her own way.

*

Jenna was glad college finished early that day and even more pleased that her client, Mrs. Goldstein, released her from her duties early. Rather than rush back to the apartment quickly, having jumped off at the bus stop, she ambled home. Outside on the front lawn she saw Leon working on a motorcycle.

"That yours?" She couldn't help herself from asking. Jenna wasn't exactly setting a shining example of keeping her distance from Leon.

"Uh-uh," he grunted, using an array of tools that seemed to be quite intricate. "I couldn't afford this beast. I'm doing this as a favor."

"For 'The Wheels Of...'" her voice dropped below audible as she recognized the logo painted on the motorbike of the notoriously violent and dangerous motorcycle club.

"Not for the club," specified Leon, rotating from his haunches to face Jenna. "For a friend. I don't know if he's part of the gang or if his workshop just can't handle the extra work today."

"It doesn't sound a safe job."

"It'll be safe if you allow me to finish the job so I can get paid by the garage. If they like my work, they may even take me on," he said hopefully.

"Not sure someone that works on vehicles provided from gangs is your best job opportunity."

"It's a job ain't it?"

Jenna could see Leon's nostrils flare as he stood to face Jenna. That was normally a sign that he was verging on angry.

"I've got to get paying work, Jenna," he explained, lightly taking both her hands in his. It was an intimate gesture but Jenna found she didn't instinctively pull away. "Not a lot of people want to take on an ex-con. You know I wouldn't be stupid enough to get involved in anything that wasn't 100% legit, but these kind of guys need to have their motors fixed, too. If I work in a garage and one stops by, so be it. Doesn't mean I'm signing up as a member and you'll be seeing me in my biking leathers tomorrow."

Jenna laughed. "I sure hope not. I'll be a curtain twitcher now, checking in on what you're wearing when you arrive and leave the block."

"I kind of like the thought of you wanting to check me out," he confessed cheekily.

"You know I didn't mean it like that."

"I'm sure you didn't mean it like that, but I was just checking."

"Well, don't," huffed Jenna.

"Ahhh, you just want to check up on me to see that I'm sticking to the straight and narrow and not breaching the terms of my parole?"

185

"Exactly."

"If you really want to do that, Jenna, you won't be able to stay away from me," he winked.

Jenna fought an urge to kick the bike. She wasn't into violence or destroying the property of others, but Leon could be infuriating and sexy at times.

"Just don't be doing favors for people with questionable ethics," she warned.

Jenna stomped upstairs into her apartment. Liana was packing her backpack while baby Zada was playing in her crib. She flopped on the couch. This phone standoff with Spencer was disappointing. He hadn't been aware of what played out after he'd dropped her off on Sunday night and that she needed support; the fact that she had not received one text or call from Spencer stung. Jenna studied her phone. Given the photos of him on Friday night, was it actually her duty to initiate contact?

"You won't be able to wish a text on there," stated Liana brutally as she jumped on the sofa next to her sister.

"I know. I was sitting here feeling affronted by the fact that Spencer hasn't bothered to call."

"Told you what he was like," muttered Liana under her breath.

"Then I realized I've been so preoccupied with this

Leon business, that I didn't ring or text to see if he got home okay that night or even to thank him for the weekend."

"You got paid for the weekend," noted Liana enviously, thinking of all the clothes her sister brought home with her.

"No, I was treated on the weekend. I'm not an escort to be paid for services."

"Well that's how it beginning to look, especially as he hasn't called you yet."

"That's where you're wrong, green-eyed girl. His family is over and he's run off his feet. Manners dictate I should've rung or texted to check on his well-being and thank him again for the lovely date." Jenna emphasized the word date. "Now if you'll excuse me, I'm going to make a call," she announced, flouncing to her bedroom.

The question is do I bring up the photos of Friday night or let sleeping dogs lie? I don't know if he did anything more than party with them. If he did then I'm hurt by the exclusion. If there was something more than he's an absolute waste of space I can't waste any more time on him.

She dialed his number. It rang five times before he picked up.

"Spencer Lawson."

Jenna had hoped for a warmer reception. She'd hoped he'd had caller ID and see it was her. His tone was formal, but not unwelcoming.

"Is anyone there?"

"Sorry Spencer, it's me, Jenna."

"Oh, hi Jenna. Everything okay?"

Not really, my ex-boyfriend's out of jail and I've seen photos of the man I'm dating with a crew of women I don't recognize, thought Jenna.

"Kind of. I was making sure you got home okay the other night."

"I answered the phone. That should tell you I'm alive and well."

"It does. I can't believe I didn't think to ring and thank you for the amazing weekend."

"You thanked me in the car," he said off-handedly.

"Right. Your family got in yesterday. How's all that going?"

"Family stuff, you know."

Jenna didn't know if she had a right to pry or ask for more details. Her phone call felt distinctly redundant.

"Have you had a thought about how we might sort something out about seeing each other this week?"

asked Jenna, repeating almost the exact same words Spencer had left with her at the airport.

"I have had an idea, as it goes."

Somehow, it was only when Jenna made herself emotionally vulnerable, that Spencer would step in to reassure her and instill confidence in the lovely words he was prone to promising when they were alone together.

"My brother, his wife and my parents are out for dinner and dancing tomorrow night, leaving me with placing my niece with the babysitter. I figured seeing Zada would be in your care, you'd be responsible for making decisions to her well-being that night. Place the kids together with our nanny and we can go out and do something."

Jenna was silent. It was a lovely offer. She knew the nanny would be one of the best, but she couldn't pretend that Liana hadn't made the comment about Zada not being left with strangers. Even as her Aunty, it wasn't Jenna's place to override the decisions of Zada's mother, however supercilious and spiteful they might be.

"Please don't tell me you too are seriously questioning the ability of our child minders?" asked an aggrieved Spencer.

"Of course not. It's just that I'm caring for Zada but I'm not her mother. It's not really my decision to make. I can put it to Liana, though."

"She made herself crystal clear when we discussed it before."

"She was ratty that night and is protective of me, that's all. If I talk to her she might change her mind."

"You don't even have to tell her," persisted Spencer. "She doesn't have to know. Zada would have company, be properly looked after and enjoy herself and we'd be free to do the same."

"It doesn't work like that-"

"Don't bother, then," said Spencer. "If your family dictates your life for you and you allow that, it demonstrates to me where I stand in your list of priorities. Perhaps you'll be keen to spend time with me when I've got a private plane booked for the Bahamas."

Jenna was shocked to hear the phone slam and the dial tone beep in her ear. Spencer clearly had quite a temper on him. How had this happened? He was angry with her when he was the one gallivanting round the country with other women on the eve of their romantic weekend. He'd barely let her get a word out in the telephone conversation. Jenna could feel her own temper flaring. She dialed Spencer back and it went straight through to voice mail.

I hate call dodgers, thought Jenna. She began composing a text of epic proportion. Her finger itched to hit send. Instead, she opted to dial Kelly.

"Yes, how can I be of counsel now?"

"Do you think it's unreasonable of Spencer to refuse to see me on the grounds that he wants to put his niece and my niece with a nanny when Liana has said she doesn't want Zada placed with a stranger?"

"If he categorically said he was refusing to see you because you won't go against Liana's wishes than I'd say he was unreasonable."

"Right, he finishes the phone conversation saying perhaps I'll be keen to spend time with him if he books us on another romantic getaway – to the Bahamas."

"I'd be well up for that."

"So would I," sniggered Jenna.

The thunderous dark cloud of Spencer ditching her because of babysitting duties came biting back at Jenna.

"What he was basically implying is that I'm using him for all the good stuff that riches can buy and have no interest in getting to know him, which just isn't true."

"I guess with someone like him, that probably is a major concern in dating."

"Whose side are you?"

"Yours," assure Kelly. "I'm merely saying sometimes

our insecurities prevent us seeing things clearly. Let's be honest. You are petrified of upsetting your mother and sister and rocking the boat. You muck in and never complain or put yourself first. You've done that for as long as I've known you. Spencer comes along and challenges that thinking and you call him unreasonable. Why instead of using Liana as an excuse, didn't you find an alternative whereby you do something nice for yourself while still fulfilling family duties?"

"Like what?"

"Why can't the two of you babysit together? Liana has nothing to moan about then and the kids should go down at a reasonable hour with the nanny, leaving you guys plenty of time to jump into bed and get to know each other."

The idea didn't just sound feasible and practical, it sounded positively enjoyable.

"Remind me why you didn't go to college?"

"Lots of common sense, but no brains whatsoever," answered Kelly matter-of-factly.

"I'm not so sure about that. You came up in seconds with a situation I probably never would have considered."

"Such flattery."

"Guess I shouldn't send this text to him then."

"What's it say?" asked Kelly shrewdly.

"Spencer. I look forward to our forthcoming trip to the Bahamas. Have you thought about which club you will be attending the night before and whether you'll be taking two or three dates this time?"

"Don't send it," warned Kelly.

"Why? He slammed the phone on me acting like I was some money-grabbing harlot."

"If you like this guy, that's a discussion to be had face to face. You're fuming right now and I completely understand that. Sending things in anger is a bad idea because you might feel significantly different when you've calmed down. I said to you earlier you don't know for sure what those photos are about. You know the paparazzi will find or make up a story to sell magazines – it's how they profit."

"He's ignoring my calls."

"Because he's calming down, too. If he's got a temper on him and he likes you he doesn't want to expose you to him when he's in a rage; especially, as I suspect, when he's settled down and realizes he's behaving like a spoilt child that can't get his own way and is being mean to the people he cares about so they hurt, too."

"What would I do without you, Kelly?"

"Probably have a cheaper phone bill," laughed her

friend as she blew Jenna a kiss down the phone to say goodnight.

Chapter Ten

"The girl is infuriating," said Spencer aloud as he terminated his call.

Rupert looked over at his brother, unsure whether he should enquire as to the problem or not. His youngest brother Spencer was clearly very prickly about the new woman in his life so he was treading on eggshells.

"You good, old chap?"

Spencer considered Rupert. He was taller and leaner than Spencer, but they shared the same dark brown eyes, square faces and curly hair. Spencer had lost the majority of his Englishisms when he moved to New York, but he noted his brother still adopted phrases from his days at world-renowned private school Eton.

He rubbed his temples. "American girls are...."

"Difficult?" guessed Rupert.

"Actually I haven't found them to be until now, but maybe that's because this is the first one I've been in a relationship with."

"I didn't think two dates constituted a relationship."

Spencer sighed. He'd said so himself on Friday night when he hit the town without Jenna, but the thought of her doing the same to him filled him with fury. He hadn't enjoyed going out by himself that night. The women frequenting the club were as adoring as ever, but he couldn't interact or converse with them. Flirting came naturally to Spencer, but anything deeper and he tended to retreat - except with Jenna. Having someone to laugh and talk to as well as have sex with, gave Spencer a sense of fulfillment.

"Perhaps not, but it's headed that way," he asserted to his brother.

"Dare I venture further into sensitive territory and ask how this Brooklyn beauty is infuriating you?"

Spencer grunted. He sat on the kitchen bench and stared at his brother. "She babysits her niece on weekday evenings. Her younger sister is a single mum and goes to night school during the week. As you can imagine, this situation makes things difficult for us to see each other aside from weekends. As you're leaving Rosie with the nanny tomorrow night, I thought Jenna could leave her niece with the nanny too and we could spend a bit of time together."

"Jenna? She has a name then?"

"I put this proposition to Jenna and she refused the idea because her sister wouldn't like the baby being left with a stranger. As if Nanny Merton isn't up to the job. We've used her consistently in America since Rosie was diagnosed and she's a qualified nurse. How can leaving a child with Miss Merton not be a sensible idea?"

Rupert looked at his brother quietly. "If you told me

you were leaving Rosie with Jenna's sister or mother, I don't think I'd be overly comfortable," said Rupert thoughtfully.

"That's different. Rosie needs special care."

"Even if Jenna's sister or mother were trained nurses to deal with Rett Syndrome, I still wouldn't like the idea. I'd want to meet them and assure myself, my wife and Rosie they're in safe, competent and capable hands. I understand what you're saying about Miss Merton's credentials, but leaving your child isn't based solely on someone who looks good on paper. It's about seeing with your own eyes and trusting your own instinct.

You've put Jenna in an awkward position. If her sister's forbidden her to this she can't just defy her. It could cause havoc at home. How much do you know about Jenna's niece? Rosie's condition might disturb her. She may only be used to family so a new face would be frightening to the baby. I know this sounds patronizing, but if it was your own child you wouldn't be blasé about the whole scenario."

Spencer discovered a spot on the floor to assist in him not having to make eye contact with his older and seriously mature brother. He sniffed and kicked his heels on the bottom of the kitchen counter.

"Put like that, I can see why there might be reservations," he conceded.

"Why don't I call Nanny Merton and arrange for her

to babysit Rosie's at yours? That way Jenna can bring her niece around, Miss Merton can do the work and Jenna's on hand if her niece needs her."

"That's not a bad idea," mused Spencer. "Only don't bother calling Miss Merton to change locations. I'll ring Jenna and tell her to come here. I can cook her dinner or something. It's not like there isn't enough spare bedrooms."

"Wouldn't you be more comfortable in your own pad? You'd know your way around the kitchen?"

Spencer wrinkled his nose. Rupert had a valid point but he didn't want the paparazzi poking round and risk being photographed with Jenna again. Conducting the early stages of a relationship in the public eye was one pressure the twosome would rather not have.

"Given how we left things on the phone, here would be better. It's neutral ground. Plus it means Rosie isn't being carted around from house to house at all hours of the night."

Rupert nodded. "That makes sense."

Spencer hopped off the kitchen bench with renewed vigor. He hated initiating phone contact with women. It made him feel open to an unsuspected attack. Spencer preferred being in control with his walls up to protect him. Having spoken to Rupert, he realized his reaction at not getting his own way with Jenna didn't put him in a good light, nor did his accusation that she was only interested in him when he had cash to spend on her. The truth was, she deserved an apology and he had some serious groveling to do. If he wasn't man enough to stand up and admit to being rash, he didn't deserve a girl like Jenna.

Spencer made his way to the guest room. He paced back and forth for some time as he scrolled slowly through his contact list. Taking a deep breath, he hit the call button for Jenna's cell phone.

"Hey, it's Jenna."

"I may have been unreasonable earlier and said things that were uncalled for and untrue."

Best to get the apologies out of the way first, thought Spencer.

"Go on."

"That was it to be honest. You've every right to be weary of leaving Zada with a stranger and it was totally thoughtless of me to tell you to lie to Liana."

"You're inviting me to the Bahamas then?" asked Jenna playfully, reminding him of the insinuation that her eye was on Spencer's wallet not his heart.

"Sadly not. I'm inviting you to a townhouse I own off Fifth Avenue. I decided to showcase my culinary skills and make you dinner."

"And when's this taking place?"

"Tomorrow, if you're still free. My family stays in the townhouse when they are visiting. As they're out, I wondered if you and Zada might visit. Rosie's nanny will be here. We could see how Zada interacts with Rosie and the nanny. If everything runs smoothly, we can let the three of them get on while we eat. That way you're here if Zada needs you, but I get you to myself if everything works out."

"My friend suggested a babysitting date. I realize it isn't cool or sexy, but it does mean we can be together. So, yeah, I'd love to come."

"Is there anything you don't eat?"

"Nothing too posh like frog's legs or snails. I'm a simple girl, really."

"I wish you were."

"Wish I was what?" asked Jenna.

"A simple girl."

Jenna's mind flew to Leon and then how she'd broach the subject about Spencer's night out without her.

"The people around me are complicated," she said truthfully. "I genuinely am a simple girl."

"Should I send a car to pick you up tomorrow?"

"I'm fine with public transport." Spencer's comment regarding Jenna only being available when overseas trips were involved still hurt, irrespective of the apology.

"Jenna, don't be like that. I said something stupid and I apologized. Let me send a car for you."

"The fact is you said it. It must've come from somewhere. You must've thought it."

Spencer fought to control his voice; the conversation was emotionally demanding. Spencer didn't really do emotions. He didn't like dredging up the past. A sorry should have been an adequate end to the matter. Now it seemed Jenna wanted to dissect the squabble.

"I said it," said Spencer carefully. He stopped; surprised an excuse didn't immediately roll off his tongue to direct the conversation back to where he wanted it to be. Forced to examine why he said it, he was able to give an honest answer. "I said it because I knew it would hurt you. Because you aren't that kind of girl, I was certain my suggesting you are driven by money would offend you. I was upset because I didn't think I'd be able to see you and I wanted to upset you as a punishment."

"I wasn't expecting you to be that honest."

"I wasn't expecting to be, myself. I said it to be mean and I'm sorry. Please accept the car."

Jenna gave it some thought. It was too easy to accept everything Spencer offered as part of his billionaire lifestyle. It was important Jenna keep two feet on the ground to remember how different her circumstances were from Spencer.

"I'll accept a car to drop me home afterward but I'll make my own way over there."

Spencer sighed. "There's no point in me arguing is there?"

"None at all," said Jenna firmly, but friendly.

"Tomorrow night then," confirmed Spencer.

*

Jenna had decided on a casually sexy outfit to wear on her babysitting date. It was time to show off her slim, toned legs in skintight black jeans with whopping great high heels to give her a few extra inches. The loose cream knit top was matched with a faux black leather bomber jacket. Twirling in the mirror Jenna decided she'd achieved the perfect look of effortlessly sexy. As she was applying some light makeup, there was a knock at the door. Surprised, given Liana had left for classes and her mother was at work, Jenna checked the peephole.

Leon was slouching comfortably on the rail outside her front door.

I really don't need this right now. Trouble is he's the kind of guy who will wait unmoving until he sees me. Better get it over and done with. She unbolted and unlocked the sturdy front door.

"You're very brave, risking my mom's temper and

my sister's tongue."

"I know your mom's at work and Li's at evening classes. Figured now would be the best time to catch you," explained Leon knowingly.

"To catch me for what?"

"Are you going to invite me in?"

"Actually now's not a good time, Leon."

"You busy or something?"

She sighed. Dealing with Leon was like peeling off a band-aid very slowly. The more sensitive she was to his needs, the longer it would take.

"I'm busy and doing something. I'm off out on a date."

"Oh." His face dropped, but only for a second. "I got a job. You were the only person I could think of to share the news with."

Leon produced a bottle of sparkling wine from behind his back. It wasn't quite champagne, but it wasn't a cheap label either. Jenna felt guilty.

"Is your mom not in?"

It sounded pathetic to her own ears suggesting he break open the bubbly with his mother. She knew he was making a concentrated effort to steer clear of his old friends because they were still tied up in illegal activities. It meant he had no one his own age if he wanted to hang out. Making new friends could be hard at the best of times. Jenna was his only link to the past that had a clean record.

"No, mom's at bingo. When I was banged up, she created a new social life and stuff. Suppose when I was safe behind bars, she didn't have to make herself available to bail me out every time I got in trouble and we know how often that was. I'm pleased for her though. It's good she's got friends and activities to do outside work."

Jenna could see the sincerity in his eyes. Her heart felt as if it were cracking. Leon was making such an effort. She should be encouraging her childhood sweetheart, not abandoning him because she'd been swept off her feet by some billionaire. She checked her watch. Because she'd declined Spencer's offer of a private car, she had to accommodate for the unavoidable delays she'd encounter on her way over to his, which meant she didn't have any time for Leon. Manners forbade her from closing the door in his face.

"Is the job with the garage that fixes bikes for that dodgy motorcycle club?"

Leon grinned. Pleased he could surprise Jenna. "No. A local place I left my CV with. The friend I did some work for put in a good word and they agreed to take me on. Not bad going, given I've been out less than a week."

"It's incredible," admitted Jenna.

"Shows you what I can do when I put my mind to something."

"It sure does."

"Feels good that it's something I can be proud of."

"I'm proud of you, too."

The hand holding out the bottle went slack, as if Jenna's words of approval were enough for Leon. "Maybe I should hang onto this for another time, when you're free to celebrate. I don't start till next Monday so there's plenty of time between now and then."

Jenna desperately wanted to remind Leon that sharing a celebratory glass of sparkling wine was not her idea of keeping their distance from one another. Then again, wasn't her career as a social worker to improve the quality of life and well being of those who needed it – and didn't Leon need that right now?

Do I follow my vocation as a social worker or force myself to only see Leon as my criminal ex-boyfriend, she wondered. *Be vague. Be noncommittal. That way, you aren't letting him down, but you aren't making him a promise you can't keep either.*

"Given we live in the same block, I'm guessing we will see each other before you start the new job."

"I'll keep the bottle on ice then." Leon stepped out of

the frame way of the front door. "You have a nice night then, Jenna. I hope he appreciates his time with you."

The comment tugged at her heartstring. She remembered Spencer confessing he'd been deliberately mean to her because he hadn't got his own way. Watching Leon walk away, she couldn't help but compare the two men.

Lost in thought, she realized she'd been staring into space for over ten minutes. She dashed inside to prepare Zada. It was inevitable she'd be late now. Rather than ring Spencer and have him reprimand her over not accepting his offer of a car, she settled for an impersonal text. With Zada set up to go, she locked up the apartment and made haste.

Fortunately, the Gods of public transport had been smiling on Jenna. She had a smooth ride and was only quarter of an hour late. Pushing the pram along Fifth Avenue, Jenna was amazed by the size of the houses. Reaching her destination, she was nervous ringing the doorbell.

Spencer opened the door in beige chinos and a maroon polo shirt and brown suede shoes. He was impossibly handsome. As he kissed her on the cheek, she felt her stomach doing flip flops. Crouching low, he extracted Zada from the pram and lifted her high in the air. Zada was laughing and gurgling. Spencer's smile was boyish as he relished the baby's joy at his antics. He landed a kiss on the top of Zada's head.

"Want to come and meet Rosie and Nanny Merton?"

Jenna wasn't sure if the question was directed at her or Zada.

"Sounds like a plan," she answered on her niece's behalf.

They traipsed up two flights of stairs to get from the kitchen situated in the basement to the nursery and main bedrooms on the first floor. As Jenna expected, Miss Merton was lovely. In her late thirties, she was warm, friendly and radiated competency and the natural instinct to care. Zada was taken with her straight away.

"You need to meet Rosie."

Jenna's hand flew to her mouth at the sight of the little girl. Her skin was the complexion of peaches and cream and she had bright brown eyes and her dark hair was cut in a bob. Rosie was a gorgeous tiny thing, but the child's wheelchair she was sitting in almost had Jenna in tears. The three-year old made eye contact with Jenna and smiled glowingly at her.

"Spencer," she cried in slow tones.

"Hey, you got my name out," he replied giving her a hug.

"Rosie has trouble remembering names?" asked Jenna

Spencer shook his head. "Speaking may not be an option for Rosie in the very near future. Children with

Rett Syndrome lose the ability to communicate verbally. When she says my name, I try and remember where I am and listen hard so I don't forget the sound of her voice when it goes completely."

"Can Zada play with her?"

"Hopefully. Rosie's alert and has an interest in her surroundings. Her motor skills aren't good, but she's quite sociable."

In her infancy, Zada's curiosity resulted in her approaching Rosie directly. Rosie was calm and sweet, and watched Zada play, reacting positively when Zada tried to involve her.

"I better get back to the kitchen or dinner will be burnt," said Spencer huskily. "Come join me if you're happy to leave Zada here."

Content that Zada and Rosie were a good match, after exchanging a few words with Nanny Merton, Jenna re-entered the kitchen.

Spencer had his back to her as he cooked. Jenna had no idea what to say.

"I'm glad I brought her."

"Who?"

"Zada. I'm glad I bought her to spend time with Rosie."

"Me too," he said shortly.

"I can see how wonderful Nanny Merton is and I can see how devoted you are to Rosie. I think it'll be good for Zada to spend time with such a sparkly little fighter with a big heart."

Spencer tuned around. His expression was a mixture of kindness and pride. "Rosie truly is something special. Going through that rapid destruction phase and somehow she's always able to make us smile."

"I know. I feel quite ashamed we had a bust up regarding when we'd be able to meet next, when there are far bigger problems in the world being faced by far smaller people."

Spencer walked to Jenna, bowed his forehead and ran his hands on her upper arms. "I know our lives are very different Jenna King, but I don't think you and I are."

Jenna could feel her heart racing. She could feel the warmth of Spencer's hands through her knitted sweater. She wanted him. It wasn't about the billions in his bank account. It wasn't about his handsome good looks. It was about a man that was as sensitive as he was intelligent and generous as he was motivated. Jenna put her hand over his heart and raised her head to meet his eyes.

Chapter 11

Spencer's brown eyes were fathomless. Jenna could feel the strong beat of his heart. He gazed at her intently, but remained rooted to the spot. Jenna lifted her head higher in order for her to brush his lips. Catching her lips, he was able to transform the kiss from a peck to something that lingered longer.

Unused to taking the lead, but drawn to the softer side Spencer had revealed in the nursery, Jenna reached her arms round Spencer's neck to drag him lower for a deeper and longer kiss. As they kissed on the tiled floor of the kitchen, Jenna's arms eventually released their loop hold on Spencer's neck. Resting on his waist, she tentatively let her hands wander the leather of his belt until she found the buckle. Trembling, she unbuckled his belt and clumsily undid the button and flies of his chinos. Her thumbs slipped inside the Emporio Armani waistband of his boxers. Spencer broke the kiss and raised his head to the ceiling waiting for Jenna's next move.

On previous encounters, it had been Spencer leading the way. Pulse racing, Jenna crouched until she was kneeling on the floor. She could see Spencer's cock pressed hard against the pristine white cotton of his underwear. As she rolled down his boxers, she was surprised at how horny she was at the sight of Spencer's naked erection. Eight inches long and thick, she licked her lips as her hand gripped his shaft.

She let her tongue flick over the helmet of his dick and was encouraged when she heard him gasp loudly. Opening wide, she imbibed the bulb and sucked hard.

Spencer bit his lip from moaning out loud, lest they draw attention to the basement. His hand went to Jenna's head. Softening her throat, Jenna was relaxed enough to start inching Spencer's rod down her mouth. Taking him as deep as possible, her head bobbed on the rock hard erection. Spencer thrust his hips slightly, which brought tears to Jenna's eyes as she choked on the shaft. Releasing him from her mouth, she used her hand to work him while her tongue tended his balls. Her touch was driving Spencer slowly crazy.

Tapping her shoulder, when she looked up Spencer nodded to insinuate that she should stand. Jenna did as Spencer wanted but kept one hand tight around the base of his cock. His eyes were half shut at the pleasure Jenna was bestowing on his dick.

Hurriedly, he lifted her top over her head. Flinging it to the ground, his hands went straight to the cups of her deep pink bra. Roughly, he shoved them down to get a view of her pert, rounded breasts. His large hands massaged them, causing Jenna to arch her back so that her breasts filled Spencer's hands. Squatting slightly, Spencer took her left nipple in his mouth. He sucked forcefully until he felt it hardening between his teeth. Releasing the nipple, he latched onto her right breast to do the same. As he took in mouthfuls of the dark flesh of her breast, his hands went to her jeans. Unlike Jenna, Spencer was quicker and more

211

confident in easing his access to Jenna. Her belt and jeans were undone in under a minute.

Spencer dropped to his knees and shoved Jenna's jeans toward her ankle with him. Carefully he undid the strap of one of her high heels. Jenna was able to use Spencer's broad shoulders to steady herself as he assisted in removing both items of footwear. Free of her heels, Jenna kicked her jeans away. Spencer laughed at her wantonness. He liked the sexy side of Jenna that wanted him in a raw and physical way.

Teasing her carnal urges, Spencer bit the sheer pink material of Jenna's briefs. As his head tussled with the cotton, Jenna was surprised to hear a rip and watch her panties magically fall to the floor. Spencer stood up and began striding forward, forcing Jenna to stumble backwards until she felt an object directly behind her.

"I told you I'd take you at a dining room table," he reminded her.

Her smile was brief. Spencer was serious. He lifted her on the table and placing a hand on her breast bone pushed her back until she was lying flat on the oak surface. Grabbing her by the ankles, he held them wide apart to permit himself a view of her perfectly groomed slit. Turned on by trimmed pussy, he thrust his cock straight into her entrance. He could feel Jenna stiffen as he worked his length into her. Legs still high and wide, Spencer was able to withdraw the eight inches and then plough straight back into her.

Taking his time, he glided in and out of her. The constant pressure of his helmet bursting through and then sliding out of her slit had Jenna writhing on the table close to orgasm. Spencer liked looking down to see his cock devoured by Jenna's needy pussy. To be in her so deep that his pubis was firm against her pussy lips was a visual aphrodisiac.

Determined to bring Jenna to climax first, he continued to tease her by sliding into her and then sliding back out. She was begging for more of him, but he knew teasing her slit would be the key to her orgasm. In minutes, Jenna was thrashing around on the table, her legs shaky in Spencer's firm grip. Her breathing was sporadic and there was no doubt in Spencer's mind he'd delivered a mind-blowing orgasm to Jenna.

Hoisting her legs over his shoulders, Spencer was able to increase his speed. Cock buried in Jenna, he slammed repeatedly into her – hard and fast. Jenna was bouncing off his pubis from the force he was penetrating her with. Dragging her by the waist further onto his shaft, he pumped furiously, enjoying Jenna's whimpering. Jenna locked her ankles around Spencer's neck to ensure he could pound her as vigorously as he demanded. With Jenna providing resistance, Spencer's hands were free to caress Jenna's breasts and roam her youthful body.

As he felt himself getting ready to release, he rammed Jenna up the table and climbed on top of her (and the table) for the last few jerks of his hips. One hand stroked her face as he balanced his weight on the other. In seconds, his teeth were gritted and his eyes shut tight as he took himself over the brink.

He lay on Jenna for a few minutes. His hot breath on her face was strangely comforting.

"How come whenever I'm with you I end up naked while you're still fully clothed?" she asked.

"Because you're too polite to tear off my clothes," he answered glibly. "But you'll learn soon enough that buttons can be sewn back on shirts and fingernail scratches on my back will heal."

She shook her head unsure of whether he was joking or not. "I hope dinner's not spoilt. I'm famished," moaned Jenna.

Spencer watched in amusement as she collected her clothes and dressed herself. She flung the ripped briefs at him. "Can't see me being able to stitch those up."

Spencer examined the handy work of his teeth. "True. Sometimes in the spirit of passion, one inadvertently sacrifices the odd item of clothes that can't be repaired. These being one of them."

"Keep them as a souvenir," she laughed.

"Why, was that the last time?" he grinned.

Jenna immediately thought of Leon. She hated that a picture of him came so easily to her mind.

"No! Of course not. I was being silly."

Jenna's voice was shrill. Spencer gave her a strange look.

"I was only joking," he said softly.

*

"I feel like we never do anything the normal way," remarked Spencer over their main course.

He was a reasonable cook. Admittedly, the antipasto bruschetta wasn't a challenge for the fledging chef, but the slow-roast pork belly with celeriac and pear mash had required his best efforts and a degree of skill in the kitchen.

"In what way?"

"We started with dessert and then went onto our entrees and main course," said Spencer by way of an example.

"There's nothing wrong with having a taste of what's to come early on. Speaking for myself, it sweetened the ambiance of the evening for me."

"It stirred something in me, but it certainly wasn't something sweet," smirked Spencer, with the devil flashing in his brown eyes.

Jenna pursed her lips in mock disapproval.

"I pay for your services to accompany me on a night

out before I even realize myself I want to date you properly. Tonight we've started blending our families when we haven't even been going out for a month."

"Not every relationship is typical or traditional. I guess if it works for us then that's all that matters."

"I suppose so," agreed Spencer absently.

Jenna was happy to see he didn't flinch when she used the word relationship. Now seemed as good as time as any to bring up his antics in the nightclub last Friday night.

"Are you aware of a magazine called 'Faces and Places'?" enquired Jenna.

"No. Should I be?"

Jenna retrieved the magazine from her handbag and slid it across the table to Spencer.

"It's a gossip rag. Why on earth would I be familiar with it?"

"There's a section in it called 'Who's About Town'"

Jenna flipped the magazine open to the pictures from last Friday night. Spencer pored over the pages for a second or two before a look of dawning realization came on his face. She could see his cheeks blushing.

"It's not what it looks like," he mumbled.

"How clichéd."

A horrible silence filled the room. Everything had been going so perfectly and now Jenna had opted to ruin it. Was it really that important? The date felt ugly and the sex felt cheap and tacky. How had something passionate and romantic distorted into something disappointing and accusatory.

"Jenna, this is new to me."

"What? Sleeping with one woman?"

"No. I've always been a monogamist. I haven't ever been keen on relationships. Dating you is a first for me."

"Okay, let me put this to you Spencer, for future reference. When you date someone, you don't ditch them when you're bored to go out and play at being a legendary lothario with some blonde-haired bimbos."

"Only one of them is blonde," pointed out Spencer.

Jenna glowered at him.

"Sorry. I was trying to make the atmosphere a little lighter."

"Maybe we didn't say we were exclusive, but why put all that effort in with me to get my schedule into some semblance of normality we could date if what you actually want to be doing is playing the field? Can you imagine how I felt when someone else brought these pictures to my attention?"

"I wasn't trying to get away from you. I felt I'd been

in chains all week because of your working hours and finding a resolution to it. I had an evening free, I knew you were babysitting and packing but I felt I needed to release some stress. I didn't purposefully go out with the intention of being photographed with those women."

Jenna was slightly relieved to discover that Spencer didn't know their names.

"You must've known you'd draw that kind of attention by going to that swanky club."

"I'm not going to lie to you. Yes, I did know I'd draw attention. I always do in nightclubs, parties, premiers and whatever else is a social setting of interest to housewives and teenagers, but I'm not going to allow that to stand in the way of me going out and having a good time."

"I get that. I guess I just wish your idea of going out and having a good time included me."

"It does," emphasized Spencer. "I went out because I was going stir crazy in the apartment. I never spend time in there by myself at night. It's lonely. The point is I went out to enjoy myself and I realized that without you, there wasn't anything to enjoy. It was far lonelier being around women I had no interest in, than being in the apartment knowing you were only a phone call away."

"I want to believe you."

"Then do! I had no idea how quickly you'd change my life, but I'm on a steep learning curve and can see the impact you've made on me. That's why we're here tonight and you're not babysitting in Brooklyn and I'm not out by myself in Manhattan trying to get laid."

Jenna turned away. It had been right to approach Spencer calmly and listen to his explanation, but the photos in the magazine hurt every time she looked at them.

"I know I should see this as a good thing. I know you're going out of your way to be open and honest with me, but something feels wrong."

Spencer pushed his plate aside and clasped her hands in his.

"Jenna, nothing feels wrong between you and me and you know that. You are not the kind of girl to jump into bed – or on a table – with just any man. Seeing that magazine is horrible, but nothing happened. Some girls wanted their photo taken and walked out with me when I exited to ensure they were published in this glossy.

We've gained something from this incident. I appreciate that I derive more pleasure from sharing an experience with you, Jenna King, than by myself. You learn not to jump conclusions and have a greater insight into the public interest my personal life attracts. It's unpleasant, but it doesn't mean something is wrong between you and me."

Jenna's cell phone buzzed in her handbag. "One second. It's probably Liana wondering where Zada and I are."

Spencer watched closely as she checked her phone. It was a text. Her face was a mask he couldn't read.

"Make time for me soon please. I could really do with a friend right now. Leon."

Jenna reread the text from Leon. His timing was impeccable in clashing with pivotal moments between her and Spencer.

"Liana alright?" asked Spencer.

"Yeah, fine."

"She's not bothered you bought Zada here?"

Jenna shook her head.

"Has she given you permission to stay the night?"

Jenna didn't have an answer to that. She hadn't even considered the possibility herself.

"I didn't ask." It was an honest answer.

"Call and ask her," pressed Spencer.

"I've got to clean early tomorrow morning and I've classes all day. I'm not sure spending the night with you would be a good idea. I can't afford to miss work and I need to be alert in lectures."

"Stay and take a car early tomorrow morning. It'll be faster and more comfortable with private transport. You'll get a good night's sleep and be on time for work."

"I don't know. I still have to get Zada home in the morning and how long do we have to wait for your parents and brother to arrive back here before we go to your apartment."

"We won't be going to my place. We'll stay in the spare room here so as not to disturb Zada's sleep. I can send Zada in the car and lend you Nanny Merton if you don't have time to go home directly. If you give Nanny Merton your stamp of approval, surely Liana won't object to that will she?"

Jenna's head felt like it might explode from the pressure. Spencer was killing her with kindness. She felt torn between her heart, which longed to stay with Spencer and her sense of duty which obliged her to return home to offer support to Leon.

"Can I ask you a question?"

"Go ahead," offered Spencer.

"Promise you'll give me an honest answer."

"You have my word."

"If you had a choice between doing the right thing for someone else or doing something for yourself that might result in hurting another person what would you do?"

"That's not a black or white question Jenna. There's a time to put yourself first and a time to put other's ahead of yourself."

"But how do you know which is which?"

"I don't think there's a textbook answer. I guess my advice would be to choose a decision that'll ensure you can sleep at night with a clear conscience."

Jenna nodded her head knowing what she had to do.

"I have to go. I can't stay tonight. I'm so sorry."

"It's fine," pacified Spencer, sensing her distress. "You know Jenna, it may sound trite, but a problem shared is a problem halved. You should know by now, I'm not a playboy billionaire without compassion or humanity. I might be able to help if you'd let me know what's going on."

"I don't know what's going on."

"Let me come with you. That way I can make sure you're okay and give a hand if you need it."

Her fingers went to Spencer's cheek and she stroked it gently. Looking helplessly in his eyes, Jenna wanted nothing more than to curl up in his arms and have a night away from her responsibilities but she shook her head instead.

"You can't come Spencer. It wouldn't be right."

His jaw tightened as though he was steeling himself to deal with the rejection. "Guess I'll stay here and wait for you."

"How long will you wait?" asked Jenna.

"However long it takes," promised Spencer.

Chapter 12

Whizzing through the streets of New York toward Brooklyn, Jenna's mind was buzzing. Her British billionaire boyfriend, Spencer Lawson, had lent the private car, complete with chauffeur, to her. If he knew Jenna was rushing back home to see her ex-boyfriend, he may not have been so forthcoming with his generous gesture.

Jenna bent sideways to check on her niece in the baby seat. She seemed content and appeared to be dozing off, thanks to the smooth ride of the chauffeur.

"I'll have to get her indoors before I visit Leon," she thought.

Staring out the windows, she tried to make sense of what was going on. Jenna had grown up with Leon – they'd been childhood sweethearts. With that kind of history, it was difficult to let go. But their youth had been misspent. Jenna possessed the good sense to get her life on track and attend NYU after high school, but Leon had chosen to become involved with a gang and ended up in jail for petty crime and drug dealing. As young lovers, they'd vowed to let one another go and turn their lives around.

Since his release, it appeared as though Leon had followed Jenna's lead and had just landed his first legitimate job as a mechanic. However, the vow to keep their distance from each other was proving hard – especially as they lived in the same block of apartments. Jenna was doing her best to keep Leon at arm's length but could see his loneliness and the struggle he was having readjusting to life outside prison.

Midway through her dinner with Spencer, Leon texted Jenna to let her know he needed to talk. Jenna sensed the urgency in his text and was relieved Spencer gave his blessing to abandon their date so she could address her problems at home.

To avoid risking a fallout with Spencer, Jenna had chosen to be vague about the details of her getaway. With Leon hounding her, Jenna didn't think she could face Spencer's wrath on top of that. Jenna was well intentioned; Leon had no friends since leaving behind his criminal past. By the sounds of things, Leon was a friend in need. Jenna was the only available and suitable person for him to turn to in his hour of need.

As a social worker in training, she felt it her duty to assist those in trouble. Deep down, Jenna knew by dropping everything to attend to Leon, she was encouraging and increasing their contact and potentially jeopardizing the foundation of her potential relationship with Spencer. With the interference of the paparazzi, a conflict with her job for the cleaning firm she worked for and Leon's early release from jail, the couple was constantly struggling to get their relationship off the ground.

They hadn't even been dating a couple of weeks but Jenna knew her reasons for dating Spencer were far deeper than physical attraction, despite his catwalk good looks. On the surface, he was dashing and charming, and came across as materialistic and something of a playboy. Having witnessed the other side of Spencer, Jenna learnt he was a philanthropist with his wealth and a devoted son, brother and uncle – especially to his niece who suffered from Rett Syndrome.

He wasn't emotionally available or particularly open, but the glimpses of his sensitivities warmed Jenna's heart. And her heart was currently thumping in her chest in an attempt to draw her attention to the fact that she may have made an error of judgment in rushing away from dinner to check in on Leon.

Why didn't I just finish the date and contact Leon later or, better yet, why didn't I tell Leon I'd visit him as soon as I was available? She asked herself quietly.

As the car pulled up at the grim and intimidating apartment block where Jenna lived, she sighed heavily. It was a far cry from the huge townhouse on Fifth Avenue where she'd been dining earlier that evening.

"May I carry the pram upstairs for you or help with the child?" inquired the driver politely, as he opened the car door for Jenna.

There was a time for independence and pride and a time to accept help. Spencer had obviously briefed the driver that the lift to her building was out of service. Struggling with the pram and baby Zada was a hassle. The driver had a friendly face.

I suppose it's what he's paid for, she thought guiltily.

"I'd appreciate that."

Taking the pram, the driver followed Jenna's direction and walked her to the front door of her residence.

"I don't mean to be ignorant, but should I tip you?" asked Jenna, embarrassed she wasn't familiar with protocol.

"Not at all, Ms. King. Mr. Lawson will be pleased to know you're home safe and sound."

Jenna smiled, but felt awful inside. She suspected Spencer had insisted the driver use the broken lift as an excuse to ensure Jenna was accompanied to her door. He was thinking of her well-being, while she'd prioritized her ex-boyfriend's problems.

Using her keys to let herself in, she was unsurprised

to see her younger sister, Liana, lounging on the sofa studying from a textbook. Her sister, however, was stunned to see Jenna home early.

"What's going on? I thought you and the billionaire would be having a sleepover."

I should be so lucky, thought Jenna.

"It didn't pan out that way," said Jenna cagily.

"Zada hated the nanny, didn't she? I told you my baby was only happy being cared for by family."

"Actually, Zada was very taken with Nanny Merton. She was playing with Spencer's niece and I didn't hear a peep from her the whole night. She was sound asleep when I left."

"Oh."

Liana went to her child. At only twenty, the burden of being a young single mother was eased by her sister's assistance with babysitting as she attended evening classes, and her mother's unwavering support by ensuring they were housed, fed and clothed.

"I suppose Spencer Lawson can afford the best care for his precious niece."

"He can," affirmed Jenna sharply, "and he has to. Rosie is not a well child. It's awful to see a little girl in a wheelchair and knowing her quality of life may not improve. Be thankful Zada is healthy and we don't have that constant pressure."

Liana looked ashamed of herself. She'd been harsh on Spencer, assuming he was using her sister as a bit of fun. In truth, he'd been perfectly polite and friendly to her – he'd even offered Liana help so that she could devote more time to her studies. In truth, what Liana didn't want to admit was that she was jealous of her sister.

She was stuck with a child and part-time education at the age of twenty, while her sister was nearly a qualified social worker with a hot, new, rich British boyfriend. Liana adored her older sister and knew she deserved the best. If Spencer made Jenna happy, then she shouldn't interfere or put up obstacles because she wasn't thrilled by her own circumstances and distinct lack of a boyfriend.

"I suppose I jumped to conclusions about the fancy rich boy."

"You did," agreed Jenna.

"Do you think it's too late to take him up on his offer to leave Zada with Nanny Merton this week while I focus on assignments?"

"Given how rude you were to him when he first gave

you the opportunity, I'd think it's very bold to call up and say you want to use his upscale nanny for free now I've given her a positive assessment."

"All the same, can I have Spencer's number?"

Jenna looked despairingly at her sister. She loved her dearly, but she could be an absolute trial at times.

"Are you going to abuse it?"

"No. I'm going to ring and apologize for being rude when he visited, and also give my stamp of approval for Nanny Merton to take Zada whenever the two of you want an evening together while I'm at college."

"Seriously?"

"Yes. And then I'm going to ask him if I can drop Zada over tomorrow morning so I can spend the day catching up on my studies."

"I'll think about it," Jenna said, rolling her eyes.

Liana was a force of nature. Sharp tongue and quick temper aside, her sister had a heart of gold and Jenna knew she wouldn't intentionally be destructive with her relationship with Spencer.

"How come you're back so early if Nanny Merton was perfect? Is Spencer an awful cook? Did he give you food poisoning and you didn't want him to hear you on the toilet?" laughed Liana.

"No. I think Leon might be in trouble."

Liana's hazel eyes made contact with her sister's. Jenna could see the disapproval in them.

"What kind of trouble and why would you want to be involved?"

The silence was thick and heavy in the two-bedroom apartment.

"Not the kind of trouble you're imagining. I told you, he's changed. He's not like that anymore."

"Then whatever problems he's got, they aren't your concern, Jenna."

"Liana, he has no one."

"He has his mother!"

"He's a...you know...Leon's not going to confide in just anyone and he's not the kind of guy to randomly ask for help. If he's reached out to me, I can't ignore him."

"You don't have to ignore him, but you don't have to drop everything at a moment's notice to go rushing to his rescue. How did Spencer feel about it?"

"He felt I should go if it meant that I wouldn't be able

to sleep tonight if I chose to ignore the cry for help."

"That was understanding of him. I'd be fuming if my boyfriend left mid-date, to go and see an ex."

"I didn't mention that part," admitted Jenna.

"Why? If you really want to keep your distance from Leon and he means nothing to you, why didn't you tell Spencer?"

"Because it's complicated," hissed Jenna.

"It's only complicated when feelings are involved."

"And feelings are involved."

Jenna put up her hand to prevent her sister interrupting.

"But not of the romantic kind," specified Jenna.

"It's your life. Do as you please. I'm younger than you, Jenna. We had the same upbringing and I rushed into the university to find the first bad boy on campus that I could: like Leon. Remember Zada's father flew the coop and I have no idea where he is to chase him for child support. He'll probably never have anything to do with my daughter. A bit like our dad, wherever he may be. Leon is weaving a web specifically for you, and your nobility and soft heartedness will get you trapped in it."

"I think you're wrong," said Jenna, slamming the door as she walked out of the apartment to find Leon.

*

Making her way to the far side of the building, Jenna was glad of the fresh air to clear her head. Some of the comments Liana had made resonated with Jenna. When she received the text from Leon, her first instinct was to help. Leon knew her inside out. He'd have accurately guessed her reaction to his contacting her and he knew she was on a date with Spencer. Had it been a calculated move on his part or merely bad timing?

She knocked on his front door. Half expecting his mother to answer, she was surprised to find the bulk of the brutish Leon greeting her.

"Hey," he said cheerfully.

He doesn't look depressed or in need of someone to talk to, thought Jenna.

"Hey yourself. Is your mom not in?"

Leon shook his head. "She's out with her girlfriends. I expect she'll spend the night with one of them." Leon stepped backward and indicated Jenna should enter the apartment.

"You asked me to make time for you and said you needed a friend. What's going on?" asked Jenna.

"Would you like a drink?"

"Sure."

"Shall I open the champagne I bought earlier?"

Jenna was going to correct him by identifying that it was only sparkling wine but bit her tongue.

"I'm not certain having an alcoholic beverage right now is the best idea if you aren't in a good frame of mind," answered Jenna delicately.

"It'll improve my frame of mind," smiled Leon.

Before Jenna could protest, the bottle was opened and she was being passed a glass.

Leon sat beside her on the sofa. He was physically close. Jenna felt mildly uncomfortable and yet she'd spent years on this very same sofa with Leon. Hell, she'd lost her virginity on that particular sofa.

"I'm glad you made time for me."

"Your text read as if you needed it."

"I do."

"As a friend," started Jenna deliberately, "what can I do for you?"

Leon downed his drink and quickly poured another. Jenna took care to sip hers slowly.

"Dutch courage," explained Leon.

"What do you need Dutch courage for with me?"

"I'm a man and I don't like talking about feelings and stuff."

"Oh come on, it's me," laughed Jenna. "Think of what we've shared over the years. One of the reasons we lasted as long as we did was because we told each other everything."

"I know, and now I'm not supposed to tell you anything."

Jenna found herself downing her glass and refilling it without invitation from Leon. This was not the conversation she was expecting and its direction was dangerous.

"Leon, you and I together was nothing but trouble. We both agreed on that and that's why we decided to go our separate ways."

"Sure, sure. We did make that pact when I was convicted. It's only that I've come out of jail and I've got no friends."

"You've landed a new job. You're bound to make

friends there. You're a likable guy. That's why it was so easy for you to con unsuspecting victims."

"I don't do that now," he reminded her.

"I know. I'm only saying that you don't even have to make an effort, people are naturally drawn to you. You've been hanging round the block since you got out. It's depressing and full of a lot of losers. You shouldn't be mingling with them. Of course, you aren't going to meet any new people until you're in a situation that allows you to do that. Work will give you that environment. "

"Jenna, men don't really discuss the kinds of topics that you and I did. That's what's made you special to me. It's not easy to find that kind of -"

"Friendship," interjected Jenna, in case he said something inappropriate.

"And now the one true friend I did have, I'm not supposed to spend time with her."

It was awkward. Even Jenna wasn't blind as to what Leon was skirting around.

"Leon, I haven't abandoned you. I haven't been rude to you since you've been back and I haven't avoided you."

"Exactly. That's why I think we should reconsider

our pact to keep our distance. We're throwing away a lot of history and maybe something more."

"Nothing will erase our history Leon but we can't live in the past."

"You don't think the fact that we grew up together and went through so much, doesn't impact on the present?"

"Of course it does. The reason we agreed we were best out of each other's lives was because we were holding each other back. Think of the progress we've made since we've been apart. My coursework has improved and I'm due to graduate at the end of this academic year.

You've started a mechanic apprenticeship in jail and have acquired a permanent job. When we were together, you were dabbling in gangland activities and I was sitting round with no inspiration or future plans. Being apart works for us."

"It worked for us," echoed Leon, emphasizing the word 'worked'.

Jenna could feel her frustration mounting. "I have to be honest, Leon, since you got out and our paths have crossed, and life hasn't been smooth sailing for me. I mean, I just left a date halfway through because I thought there was something seriously wrong with you."

"There is something seriously wrong," growled Leon. "You left your billionaire boyfriend to come see me. What exactly does that tell you? If you wanted nothing to do with me, you'd have steered clear. You certainly wouldn't run out on a date to visit me at my place." Leon was passionate and his argument was convincing.

"That's not how it was," argued Jenna.

"Are you sure?"

"Yes, I'm sure. I came because I was worried about you, but if anyone sent a text with the same degree of urgency as yours, I'd be inclined to go to them straight away."

"Why didn't you call me to see what was wrong?"

"Why am I under interrogation here?" snapped Jenna. "I did you a favor by coming round. I thought you were struggling. I thought I might be able to help."

"I am struggling. I'm struggling to see why you won't let me back with you."

"Because it's wrong. Because I've moved on," she shouted.

Her raised voice echoed throughout the apartment.

From the corner of her eye, Jenna could see Leon was visibly upset.

"I've changed, you know."

"I know that," she said quietly.

"You've changed, too."

"Yes, I have, Leon."

"We're both in completely different places to where we were when we agreed it was best to part ways. Given the strength of our relationship and how long we were together...don't you think it's worth reconsidering? Isn't it worth seeing how we work together now we've matured and have similar desires for the future?"

Jenna felt trapped. Objectively, Leon had a very valid point. She'd barely been with Spencer. It was all still very new. They were only arguing a few hours earlier about his recent tryst in a club and whether their relationship was exclusive. It's not as though she was in so deep that she couldn't get out. Her phone beeped. It was a text from Spencer.

"I hear you got home safe and sound. Hope everything's okay at your end. Call me if you need anything. In the meantime, I'll call tomorrow and maybe we can find a time to meet up and finish that date."

She smiled at the correct grammar and lack of abbreviated words in his texts. She'd been so flustered by her interaction with Liana, and tense about seeing Leon, that she completely forgot to let Spencer know she was home.

You didn't even think to thank him for the car or dinner, she thought glumly.

A small smile crept over her face as she remembered how quickly Spencer was to apologize, explain his actions when he'd insisted she go on a date with him, and negate her babysitting duties. Spencer had manners and integrity. Even in the text, there was nothing to pressure her into revealing her whereabouts or what situation demanded her immediate presence.

On the surface, it might be easy to walk away from Spencer and try again with Leon. The past was always safer than the future; the familiar always easier than the unfamiliar. The trouble was, Jenna was in too deep with Spencer. She had no inclination to walk away from him. Her relationship with Leon was based on obligation and duty, not out of genuine feelings. Her generous heart made her the kind of girl to rush in and help anyone in trouble, but that was where this visit started and stopped – it had nothing to do with her secretly wanting to be with Leon. The difficulty arose in how to communicate that sentiment to Leon.

"Leon, I understand you're hurting and I actually appreciate your reasons for wanting to spend time together, but when I say I've moved on, I mean emotionally and not just in my day-to-day life. You've come out of prison and your world has transformed. It's hard to get your head around it. Humans are creatures of habit. Wanting to be with me is nothing more than you wanting something secure and stable while you get back on your feet. It'd be a disaster using that as a basis of a relationship."

"You've got all the psychobabble, Jenna, and I'm sure your lecturers applaud your ability to theorize my behavior, but you're wrong. I've loved you for forever and that's never going to change."

"I suspect in time, you'll find you're wrong there. I loved the boy I grew up with and I have huge admiration and respect for the man in front of me, but I'm not in love with you. If you believe you have those feelings for me, Leon, then I'm convinced we absolutely need to stay away from one another, properly this time. No conversational pleasantries. No stopping by to check in on me or share in a celebratory drink. I promise you, you'll start enjoying life again and realize you don't need me by your side to have a good time."

"You're wrong," contradicted Leon. "Think long and

241

hard before you walk out that door, Jenna."

"Leon, are you threatening me?"

"As I'm sure one of your clever textbooks would've told you, there are consequences to your actions and you walking out of here will have repercussions."

"That is not how friends behave toward one another," asserted Jenna as she made her way to the front door.

Chapter 13

For once, Jenna was relieved her part-time job required an early start. Even though the apartment block was ghostly quiet, she felt on edge as she left home. Liana had waited up for Jenna's return from visiting Leon the previous night, but Jenna knew better than to confide in her..

Liana lacked any discretion whatsoever. If Jenna told Liana about Leon's request and subtle threat, Liana would run straight to their mother to inform her. Their mother, Hannah, held down three jobs and she already blamed the necessity of her excessive hours at work as being solely the result of Jenna's wayward past and Liana's accidental pregnancy. If her mother discovered Leon was actively trying to make a place for himself in Jenna's life, it would add excess worry to a woman who was doing her best (and succeeding) to support two children and a grandchild. Jenna had no intention of adding yet another burden to her mother's shoulders.

Silent and lost in thought, Jenna felt guilty that she neglected to converse with her elderly client as she cleaned the expensive Greenwich apartment. As she made her way to NYU, she was considering exactly what damage Leon could possibly inflict on her that would seriously affect her life.

She may not have been strictly truthful, but she hadn't lied to Spencer or betrayed him in any way, so Leon couldn't be divisive in attempting to break up her new relationship. As he was starting a new job the following week, he wouldn't have the time to loiter around the block harassing her. Given the close community spirit of their block of apartments, he couldn't harangue or disturb their household without serious ramifications.

Yet there had been something in his tone of voice that suggested he could make things difficult for her if she refused to include him in her life. The episode niggled at her, mainly because she had no idea what card Leon thought he had to play that gave him power over her.

As she sat in her first lecture of the day, frustration began to set in. Everyone had warned her Leon was bad news and she'd refused to listen. She was convinced he was a changed man and had defended him to the hilt, only to find he was prepared to stoop low in order to get his own way. In times of trouble, she tended to revert to her best friend, Kelly, but Jenna could already envisage the criticism of her friend upon hearing that she'd spent one-on-one time with Leon in an unsafe environment.

Her phone vibrated in her tote bag. Usually she'd ignore it, knowing it was rude to use her phone during classes, but she was desperate to hear something comforting from one of the people close to her. Withdrawing the cell phone, she saw Spencer's name flashing on its screen. Relief washed over her. He was cool and distant but Jenna always felt safe in his presence. It was the ultimate in bad manners, but Jenna collected her laptop and textbooks and sneaked out of the classroom.

The phone had stopped ringing by the time she'd scuttled out. Finding a quiet place under a large, leafy tree, Jenna returned his call.

"Hello Jenna," answered Spencer warmly.

"Hi. Sorry I missed your call. I was in class."

"Please don't tell me you excused yourself to ring me back."

"As a matter of fact, I did. I needed to hear a friendly voice."

Spencer was quiet. Jenna's openness always caught him off guard. She was alerting him to the fact that she had a problem, but more importantly, she was drawing his attention to the reality that she considered him to be a positive and calming influence.

"I take it your emergency last night wasn't easily resolved."

"You could say that."

Spencer knew from the tone of her voice she was seriously worried, but Jenna seemed determined to keep the matter private. If he asked for further details, she might think him nosy or interfering.

"I'm sorry to hear that. I'd offer to help, but as I have no idea what's going on, I don't really have a lot of advice to give."

It crossed Jenna's mind that the reason she was reluctant to confide in Spencer was that deep down, she knew she hadn't behaved honorably. She knew the second she met Leon on the steps and stopped to talk to him, that he was keen to ignite the old flame. Call it naiveté, but she'd hoped Leon's alleged need to win her back would fade naturally over time. Instead, it had increased dramatically.

"It's nothing I can't handle," she lied. "And truthfully, it'd be of no interest to you."

"Do you actually know me well enough to decide what is, or isn't, of interest to me?"

"In this case, I do," said Jenna firmly.

There was no point in pressing the matter but Spencer was annoyed. It was as if Jenna wanted him on a leash to prevent his partying lifestyle but wasn't willing to include him in her day-to-day dramas. He was beginning to feel like a toy; someone Jenna could pick up and put down as she chose at whim. She was keeping him on the outskirts of her life, treating him like a spare part but then acted wounded when he went out without her.

"You can't have it both ways, Jenna." His voice was hard. This was not the friendly call she wanted.

"What do you mean?" she asked, with a quiver in her voice.

"You reprimand me for going to a nightclub without you when I was snapped with some fellow female attendees and then keep me in the dark regarding what's going on at your home. If it wasn't for your sister, I wouldn't have a clue about what was going on."

Jenna's temper was flaring. She could not believe Liana would ring Spencer. Her sister had asked for his number but she'd never got round to giving it to her.

She must've taken it from my phone when I was asleep, thought Jenna. *What exactly has she told him?*

"I take it Liana was seeking to take you up on the offer of a babysitter?"

"Indeed she was."

Jenna detected a note of amusement in Spencer's voice and was glad Liana had appealed to his good nature.

"I'm sorry about that. Liana has a tendency to open her mouth without thinking. One second she'll berate you for the mere suggestion that her baby should be left in a stranger's care, the next it'll be the most inspired idea she's ever heard. I didn't even pass your number onto her."

"She did say she had to stay up late until you fell asleep before she could access your contact list."

Jenna huffed in outrage. "Why she insists on behaving like a teenager is beyond me."

"She's young at heart. I guess with the baby, she had to grow up quickly. I don't think it's wholly unexpected that she'll revert to teenage behavior once in a while if she missed out on a portion of those years because she was nursing an infant."

Spencer's balanced view softened Jenna's heart. He had a valid point. Her mother was determined the household ran on a routine and it worked, but Liana must miss her freedom and the spontaneity of being young and silly at times.

"I take it Nanny Merton now has Zada."

"She certainly does."

"I'll be interested to see whether Liana actually uses this break to study or whether she'll squander it catching up with friends."

"I'm not bothered either way," laughed Spencer. "As long as it gives her a taste of freedom and a little respite, I'd say taking Zada off her hands for a few days is a good thing."

Since when did they become best friends? thought Jenna. *The last time they were together Jenna had used his credit card to order the entire menu off the local pizza joint and Spencer ended up storming out of the apartment in a mood.*

"It's very kind of you," mumbled Jenna, she wasn't sure what to say.

"Anyway, she explained you were helping an informal patient, in respect of your social work studies, and that you'd bitten off more than you can chew with the client."

Jenna sent a silent thank you to her quick thinking sister. It wasn't an outright lie and it did highlight the salient points of her predicament with Leon.

"That's a pretty accurate description."

"Social work is definitely not my area of expertise," said Spencer. "I'm guessing you have a supervisor or someone you can speak to with any problems you encounter."

"Through the university, yes, but as Liana said, this is a favor to someone I used to know. I'm not in a position to approach my supervisor regarding the case. It may look bad that I'm not doing it through the university. I'm not actually qualified yet."

"That is problematic."

Jenna could feel tears pricking her eyes. She wanted to blurt everything out to Spencer, but as he'd expressed concerns previously that she had an attachment to a convicted criminal, she knew better than to speak out.

"Are you in danger?" asked Spencer slowly.

Again, Jenna couldn't answer. Leon hadn't done anything untoward yet, she definitely felt disconcerted by his words last night.

Spencer was trying the understanding boyfriend role, but it wasn't working out for him. As a businessman, , and someone with the money to get what he wanted whenever he wanted it, not being in control or informed of his circumstances did not sit well with him.

"Is this to do with patient confidentiality?"

Jenna could hear his tone of voice rise. She knew she

was being obstructive but she'd backed herself into a corner. The one thing she didn't want to do, was lie to Spencer, thus silence was her best option at this point in time.

Spencer sighed.

"I told you the other day I wasn't the relationship type of man and that I didn't have a lot of experience in dating the same person for a period of time. But my understanding is, in order to make a relationship work, you have to trust one another. That means letting each other in and actually talking. One-sided conversations are futile."

"I know, but this situation doesn't warrant your involvement."

"I'm going to respect your word on this, but I'm also going to tell you I'm very unhappy. I understand the nature of your work, but I'm not asking for names and addresses. I merely want to know what is going on and if you're okay. I don't think that's unreasonable."

"There's nothing more I can expand on other than what Liana said."

"Fine," he said shortly. "It might've been nice to hear it from you rather than your sister."

"Liana has a habit of getting in there first."

"I hope your day improves. I need to get on with work and you need to return to your class."

Spencer's voice reminded her of one of her high school teachers.

"You're right," agreed Jenna, unwilling to let her hurt show. "Can I call you later?"

"I'm out tonight," said Spencer. "You probably won't be able to contact me. Call tomorrow, if you want."

*

"You do know you're acting like a stalker, right?" asked Kelly as she slid into Jenna's booth during her afternoon break.

"Yes, I know," replied Jenna, without looking up from her computer screen.

"Who googles their boyfriend to find out his whereabouts the previous night?"

"A person dating one of New York's most eligible bachelors."

"And has any incriminating evidence turned up in images of Spencer being surrounded by a bevy of beauties last night?"

"No." Jenna's smile was wide with relief.

"What'd you end up doing yourself?" inquired

Locked myself in the apartment with the lights out, in case Leon decided to pay me a visit, thought Jenna.

"Not a lot. It was weird. Liana ended up leaving Zada with the nanny all day and didn't pick her up until after she'd finished her classes. It's the first week-night in ages I can remember having free to myself."

"And despite that being the very situation you and Spencer were hoping for, you didn't end up going out with him."

"No," replied Jenna curtly.

Kelly twirled her blonde hair through her fingers, hoping to read her childhood friend's expression. "I don't understand you, Jenna. At first, you moan because Spencer behaves as though you're an escort and is incapable of treating you like a real person because you're his cleaner. So he goes out of his way to alter your circumstances, to put some equality in the relationship, and you become borderline resentful of his attempts to ingratiate himself with your family."

"I understand I'm being unreasonable. It's just with Leon and everything; it wouldn't be fair to let Spencer into the madhouse."

"There shouldn't be anything with Leon."

"There isn't."

Kelly wasn't used to Jenna snapping at her. Jenna always looked pretty and well-groomed but today her eyes were puffy from lack of sleep, her skin was pallid and her clothes were rumpled as though they hadn't seen an iron.

"If you told me what was going on, maybe I could help."

Jenna cracked her knuckles. Everyone was saying that -- from Spencer, to her mother and sister, and now her best friend. They couldn't help. Leon wasn't the kind of guy you crossed and Jenna didn't want to place anyone close to her in the firing line. At the same time, the constant questioning was making her irritable.

"Kelly, there's nothing to worry about. There's a lot going on in my life right now and I'm not coping well."

"As long as you know I'm here if you need me."

Jenna grabbed her friend's hand and squeezed it. "I do and I'm grateful. I think everything will settle in time. I'm stressed, but it'll pass. I promise."

Kelly feigned belief in her friend's words, but she had grave concerns about Jenna's well-being.

Watching Kelly return to her duties at the diner, Jenna took her phone from her jacket pocket.

"U & and I need 2 speak. Let me no whens good. If I dont hear back Ill come round 1 evening 2 talk."

The text from Leon made her sick to her stomach. After over a year of spending her nights babysitting Zada and living in a cramped house, Jenna should be relishing a few nights in the apartment by herself but she was petrified of going home. Frightened as to when Leon might "come round" and terrified at what the "talk" would consist of.

Sneaking into her apartment, she had the doors locked and lights out by 7 pm. She settled in bed to study a textbook by the lamp of her bedside table. At 8 pm, the doorbell rang. Startled, she froze, not moving. There was a loud, persistent knocking on the door. Her phone began ringing and Jenna realized a scream was rising in her lungs. She answered her cell phone.

"It's Spencer. Are you out tonight? I came around to see you in case you wanted company, given you're home alone."

Jenna jumped out of bed and ran to the front door. She turned on the lights as she fled through the apartment and opened the door. Flinging her arms around him she held him tight.

"That's quite a welcome, given I only brought Chinese," he said, extracting himself from her enthusiastic embrace.

"Why are you here?"

"An attempt to be romantic. Although I doubt that historically, chow mein and fortune cookies will be classed as one of the world's most romantic gestures."

"No, but a spontaneous visit comes close."

"Zada and Rosie are asleep at the town house and while I do love having my family stay, I also miss your company."

Jenna was touched by his arrival. Spencer had gone to great pains to highlight their different backgrounds and yet again, he'd made the trip to Brooklyn to spend time with her.

An appearance by Leon could cause havoc but Spencer's masculine presence had Jenna feeling safe and able to relax.

After eating, the couple collapsed on the couch.

"There are no leftovers for your sister. She won't be happy," chuckled Spencer in relation to Liana's insatiable appetite.

"It'll do her good to skip the junk food," mused Jenna.

They sat in comfortable silence.

"Is it weird for you?" asked Jenna.

"What?"

"Sitting here in this crummy two-bedroom apartment watching TV on a screen that's ten years old."

"First of all, this apartment is cozy and not crummy. It's a nice living space for a family. Secondly, unless you're obsessed with gadgets, high definition and extreme sound systems, most TVs are the same, regardless of age."

"You didn't answer the question."

"I wouldn't say it's weird. It's a new experience but I like it. It beats going out every night of the week. It becomes monotonous attending a club or function every night. I barely spend time in my apartment other than to sleep."

"As long as Nanny Merton's babysitting Zada, we should spend a few nights in your apartment doing this so I can learn to appreciate gadgets, high definition, and extreme sound systems," hinted Jenna.

The thought of sharing his living space with someone

permanently did not appeal to Spencer in the slightest.

"I was talking to Liana about that."

"Were you?"

"Liana wants a weekend off and thought she'd leave Zada at the townhouse for a few days and nights. She's planning on treating herself to a little quality time alone to pamper and preen without having to worry about her coursework and assignments. As that frees you of your responsibilities as Aunty, I wondered if you and I might spend the weekend together."

The idea of hitting the exclusive restaurants and nightclubs in New York and enjoying a weekend in Spencer's luxury apartment sounded like heaven. There'd be no worrying about Leon getting in touch with her there.

"I'm definitely available for that."

"Great. I had an idea we might go to Maine for a long weekend. We could head over there after you finish school Friday night and come back Monday morning, or Sunday evening if you can't change your work hours on Monday."

"Maine? Really?"

"It's quite beautiful there, very picturesque. I know a perfect little guesthouse in Portland. It'll make a nice break from New York City."

It sounded idealistic and Jenna couldn't fault the effort Spencer was making. However, part of her felt disconcerted that since the night of their first date at the charity gala dinner with Jenna spending the night at Spencer's apartment, she hadn't been welcomed back to his home or invited out publicly with him as his date.

You're being paranoid, Jenna, she told herself. *This whole business with Leon has you on edge. It's messing with your head. Don't be a spoiled t brat and don't let Leon's threat ruin your time with Spencer.*

As keys rattled in the door, Spencer and Jenna unwrapped their limbs to take a formal seated position on the couch. Hannah, Jenna's mother, walked inside with a huge smile on her face at the sight of Spencer.

"I bet you were hoping I was Liana," she said directly to Spencer.

Spencer smiled and stood to shake her hand and introduce himself.

"Spencer Lawson. It's nice to meet you, Mrs. King."

Hannah laughed throatily. "I bet you're thinking it's

way too early to meet the parents."

Spencer ran a hand through his brown curls and grinned sheepishly.

"Well, now you've met the whole family so there's no need for you to feel like a guest or that you have to sneak off before we're due back. I don't bark and I don't bite. Treat my girl right and we'll get along famously."

"I'll do that, Mrs. King."

Hannah set on the recliner and let herself stretch out. "Call me Hannah. You make me sound ancient calling me Mrs. King."

"My apologies. I was trying to be respectful."

"Respect is good. Friends and family is better. Do you know how to make coffee, Spencer?"

"Yes, of course."

"Then run to the kitchen and make this exhausted cleaner a cup of white coffee with two sugars."

Feeling he couldn't refuse the request, Spencer stood up and took slow steps toward the kitchen. Jenna smiled at his awkwardness. She suddenly recalled that Spencer had a coffee machine in his house that did percolated coffee, cappuccinos and lattes. This was not a piece of kitchen equipment that the Kings possessed. She bolted into the kitchen to Spencer.

"We don't have your fancy kitchen set up," she said apologetically.

Spencer looked confused as to how he'd fulfill Hannah's simple instruction.

"Stop looking stressed. She only expects instant coffee," giggled Jenna.

Spencer turned on the kettle on and watched Jenna scoop out a teaspoon of instant coffee, two teaspoons of sugar and a dash of milk to a mug. As the kettle whistled, she added the boiling water and gave it a thorough stir. She pushed the drink toward Spencer.

"You're a computer genius. Making Mom an instant coffee is simple."

Spencer took the mug and politely gave it to Hannah.

"You've been in my kitchen?" quizzed Hannah.

Spencer nodded.

"Good. The kitchen is the heart and soul of our household and you've made yourself part of that now."

Hannah crooked her finger for Spencer to come closer. He bent down toward her and she kissed his cheek. "You're welcome here any time, Spencer and when you are here, you treat this place like home."

Moved by the unexpected heart of the woman Spencer was at a loss for words. Fortunately, Liana chose that moment to burst through the door with Zada in tow. "Thanks for lending me the driver, Spencer. He's waiting downstairs to take you home when you're ready."

"I should go," said Spencer, excusing himself from the female dominated apartment.

"I hope we haven't scared you off," called Hannah.

Spencer stopped from escaping quickly out the open door. "Quite the opposite, Hannah," he winked.

Jenna rolled her eyes at his flirtatious manner. "You're terrible," she whispered as they kissed by the door.

Jenna stayed outside until she saw Spencer hop in his usual car and drive off. As she turned around to go in, her cell phone sounded an alert.

"He needs 2 go if we're going 2 make this work. Fix it or I will," read Leon's text.

Jenna scanned the lawn and lit area of the corridor to see if she could spot Leon. Her eyes couldn't detect any shadowy forms. Walking inside, she shuddered as she locked the apartment up for the night.

Chapter 14

She knew it was silly and shallow, but Jenna was filled with glee to see Spencer's stretch Hummer waiting in the NYU parking lot on Friday afternoon. Yet again, they were headed to JFK airport to take Spencer's private charter plane to Portland. Boarding the plane, a sense of relief washed over her, knowing there was no way Leon could reach her over the weekend.

The flight was a little over an hour. Disembarking, Jenna saw a silver convertible Aston Martin parked in a hangar. The jangle of metal made her head swivel and she saw Spencer dangling the keys.

"Do I get to drive?"

Spencer laughed uproariously. "Jenna, I'm a modern man, but no. In this case, I'm a traditionalist and I'll be serving you this weekend. Besides this classic British sports car needs a British man behind the wheel."

Jenna pulled a face. "It's just a car."

"Now, it's comments like that which demonstrate to me you have no appreciation of this vehicle. There's no way I'm playing passenger while you drive this beast round Portland like a grandma."

"You're being very rude."

Spencer kissed her briskly. "I'm teasing...but you aren't going to drive," he laughed as he slung her suitcase in the boot of the car.

Jenna didn't put up an indignant feminist argument. If he wanted to play chauffeur, it suited her. Truthfully, she wouldn't have felt comfortable driving such an expensive car. Her nerves would probably end up causing her to have an accident and given Spencer's love of motor vehicles, she might not prove to be a popular guest for the weekend if she had a mishap while driving.

Driving through Portland, Jenna was able to appreciate the beauty of the New England region. The scenery was similar to a picture postcard. The Old Port was an authentic working waterfront and Jenna was mesmerized by the boats and fishermen by the wharf. The cobblestoned streets and historic buildings gave the town a sense of something magical where the past and present collided. As Spencer drove toward a historic Victorian house painted blue with white trimmings on the verandah, Jenna realized how romantic the getaway was.

After being greeted by the owners of the inn and shown to their suite, Jenna was finally able to find some words of thanks.

"This place is incredible. I've never seen anything like this. Everything is so old, but so pretty."

"It's over a hundred years old," Spencer informed her. "Although I hope the bed isn't. I don't want the springs squeaking all weekend."

Jenna threw a pillow at him. "What's the plan, then?"

Spencer studied her. It was too easy to fall into the habit of having sex followed by a post coital chat. As hot as the sex was, Spencer found spending time with Jenna rewarding in a different way.

"Do you eat seafood?"

"I do," confirmed Jenna.

"As this is a seaside town and the collection of restaurants has developed a respected reputation, I would suggest taking you out for dinner to taste something fresh from the sea."

Jenna suddenly felt insecure about what she'd packed. In Paris, she'd been given the opportunity to shop for a few suitable outfits for their weekend. This time, Spencer had made no such offer and Jenna had been forced to handpick from her limited wardrobe. Freshening up in the bathroom, she had reservations about her dress. The long sleeved blue dress with a scoop neck came just below her knees. The material clung to her petite frame.

As she assessed her reflection, wishing the dress showed off more cleavage and deciding that the long sleeves and sensible length made her look like a schoolteacher, Spencer knocked and entered before she could say she was decent.

"That color suits you," he said kissing her cheek as he began to brush his teeth. "It's a good choice. It'll be cool out tonight; you wouldn't want to be wearing something skimpy."

He slicked back his hair and untucked his shirt. Jenna wanted to slap him for being so sexy. He wore white trousers, a blue striped shirt and navy blazer. Looks-wise, she felt inferior beside him, but Spencer had a way of making her feel as if she belonged on his arm.

Portland by night was something special. As Spencer linked hands with Jenna to make sure the cobblestones didn't have an argument with her high heels, she realized she was becoming less and less self-conscious in his presence.

Spencer chose the restaurant. Jenna wasn't used to eating out and was in awe of the silver service and décor of the restaurant.

"Do you remember telling me about the obstacles we'd face because of our different backgrounds?" she asked Spencer, mid-meal.

"I do."

"Has your opinion changed on that at all?"

"Are you worried I'm the kind of man who won't admit when he's wrong?"

Jenna laughed. "No. I was just thinking about us and how I feel when I'm with you and wondered how you feel when we're together."

"I believe we possibly will face obstacles because of our backgrounds and I stand by that statement, but I don't believe our backgrounds actually impact on how you and I interact with one another."

"Can you say that in plain English?"

"I think you and I have the ability to blend in with one another's lifestyles. I was wary about developing any kind of relationship with your family, but I like the dynamic of your household. I see the value you put on your family ties and it is in line with my feelings about family. Thus, what you call a crummy apartment, I call a home.

You get an emergency text from a patient that needs you and you prioritize that, I invest a lot of my time in charity work. What I'm saying is even though we live and work in different environments, I'm learning that we share the same core values and I suspect we want the same things from life."

"You hide your generosity and instinct to help people though," observed Jenna.

"I do. The business world is harsh. The traits we were talking about are often seen as a weakness in my industry. My business is important to me. I can't afford to have partners and rival firms view me as a weak link. It can be harmful to what I set out to do when I started my company. I employ over a thousand people. If investors and colleagues don't trust me to operate my business with profit as the overall objective then I put a lot of people's jobs at risk."

"I guess when I heard you were a billionaire, I assumed money wasn't a problem for you – life wasn't a problem for you."

"Money isn't a problem for me, but I have the responsibility of ensuring people are employed to provide for their families and that requires attention and care. As for life not being a problem, you've met Rosie. You know there's no cure. That reality stays with me every day and it's a problem without a solution."

"Listening to you speak, I guess we do have a lot in common. Mom, Liana and I juggle jobs and responsibilities to provide for the family and ensure Zada has a good upbringing."

"And your work?"

"I'll never make an impact on people the way you do. I'll never be able to help people or charities on the scale that you can. I can't create or maintain jobs for people to give them an income and purpose in life. I can't be a patron to specialist charities, but I do want to contribute to society."

"Social work is hands on. There's a lot of emotional labor involved and you will directly change people's lives. They'll have a face and a person to thank when their lives improve. Don't do yourself a disservice because you don't have billions in the bank account. More people will remember the work you do than the work I've done."

Dinner and dessert finished, the couple began to amble back to the guesthouse.

Spencer was quiet for a time. "You changed my life," he said boldly into the still of the night.

"How'd you figure that?"

"I made a decision to put family first and use my company as a means of giving something back to the community. It's worked well for me because it's predictable, simple and controllable. Nothing unexpected. It's safe and secure and stable. In that knowledge, I felt in my spare time I could do as I please and treat people how I wanted to, because I could justify my contribution to society.

I spend all day chancing risks at work, but when it really matters...when it comes down to the real me, alone without my wealth or reputation to fall back on, I tended to present myself as a cardboard cutout, the playboy that won't settle down. It's such an easy role and requires very little effort."

"It's nice to hear you being honest about yourself."

"Being with you, understanding you, the decisions you make, your reactions to your family, your commitment to your studies, is a real challenge. Every time I unearth a piece of the real Jenna King, it's like a part of me comes alive. I wonder what it would be like to throw away my mask and follow my real dreams.

The dreams that aren't set in stone and may not last or even come true. I watch you chasing your dreams, never knowing if they'll come to fruition and I admire your bravery. I'd like to give myself that chance to pursue personal happiness, but that would mean adopting an attitude that embraces risk and uncertainty."

"Did I change your life by inspiring you to pursue personal happiness, or because having me by your side made you realize that I gave you a degree of happiness in your life?"

Spencer pointed toward the driveway ahead of them. "We're home," he said huskily, shutting his eyes and closing his mouth on hers.

*

Jenna had never felt closer or more connected to Spencer. The minute they were in their bedroom, her hands were unbuttoning his shirt. Although pale, Spencer's bare chest was broad and pumped. Reaching the lower buttons of his shirt, she was able to view his rippled torso and flat stomach. Her tiny hands stroked his muscular upper body. As she let them move upward, she pushed his shirt and blazer off. Topless in the dim light of the room, Spencer looked like a Greek Adonis. The moonlight reflected off his partly naked frame.

Stepping closer to him, Jenna tilted her head, opening her mouth slightly, waiting for Spencer's tongue to make contact with her own. His lips crushed down on hers and he let his tongue explore her mouth before sucking on her tongue.

Prominent shoulder blades and soft skin -- Jenna's hands were exploring Spencer's sinewy back. The more intense the kiss became, the more tempted Jenna was to run her hands down his back. The electricity of the kiss and Spencer's erection pressing against her stomach through his trousers caused Jenna to drag her fingers down Spencer's back. He stiffened as she scratched his skin in an attempt to draw him closer.

There was just enough room in the waistband of Spencer's trousers for Jenna to slip her fingers in. Spencer's breathing became heavier as he felt her fingertips graze across his pubic hair. His hands went to his belt buckle to finish undressing himself. Jenna slapped them away. Placing her hands on Spencer's pecs, she pushed hard, inclining him to start walking backward. Feeling the edge of the bed behind him, Spencer sat down on the mattress and lay back.

As he expected, Jenna was hungrily undoing his belt and unzipping his fly. His hard-on was so prominent that when freed from the pressure of straining against his trousers, he groaned aloud. Jenna tugged his trousers low so they wouldn't interfere with her mounting him. Her hands were cool on his naked skin and while he enjoyed her appreciation of his toned body, there was only one place he wanted her hands to be and Jenna was deliberately avoiding it.

Spencer went to remove his tight black boxers. Again, Jenna prevented him from doing so with a hasty grip on his wrists to impair him from sliding them down. Spencer placed his hands under his head. It was torture of the sweetest kind. Jenna was increasingly turned on by the outline of Spencer's erection against his shorts. She laid a hand on the shaft and rubbed it firmly through the material. The simple motion had his cock throbbing under her touch and had her crotch damp. Her hand tightened around his length and she noticed his buttocks tensing in anticipation. Taking her time, Jenna rolled down his boxers until his eight-inch prick was exposed. It was rock hard and stood straight up. Jenna noticed a droplet of clear liquid from the slit of the helmet of his cock. Grabbing his hard-on firmly, she let her tongue run over the head to taste divine fluid. Squeezing the bulb hard, she sucked and let her tongue burrow into the slit to taste more of him.

Jenna became aware her panties were dripping wet with desire. Her need to ride Spencer's powerful cock became overwhelming. Quickly and quietly, she slipped out of her panties and stepped out of her shoes. Though tight, the material of her dress was flexible enough for Jenna to pull it up to mid-thigh. Shortening the dress gave her the freedom to climb on Spencer and straddle him.

Raising herself slightly, her hand took Spencer's dick and she guided it to her entrance. Very slowly she began to sink down on the thick shaft. His girth was commendable and Jenna was forced to stay still for a minute or two as her pussy became accustomed to the width and length of Spencer's erection. As she became more comfortable, Jenna began to roll her hips in a circular motion. She could see Spencer's eyelids fluttering in pleasure at the subtle movements.

Gradually, Jenna built up the pace and began rocking on his erection. The slightly more vigorous action tempted Spencer to place his hands on Jenna's breasts. He tugged at the dress, hoping to free them so he could view them as they bobbed in time with her bouncing. Jenna put her hands on his to stop him pulling and spoiling the shape of her dress or stretching the material.

She placed his hands firmly on her breasts indicating that was the only access he'd be having that night. Spencer squeezed hard. He heard Jenna gasping and guessed it was what she wanted him to do. He roughly grabbed and tugged her breasts. The sensation had Jenna riding Spencer faster and grinding her clit against his pubis to create a friction to bring her to orgasm.

Feeling the electric tingles begin to originate from her bud, Jenna took the opportunity to adjust her position to prolong the sex. She adopted a squatting position. Replacing Spencer's shaft back into her pussy, Jenna was able to rise and fall on Spencer's rod at her own pace. At times, she lowered herself until she was sitting directly on him, other times she imbibed only two of three inches of his cock.

Frustrated, Spencer's hands went to her tiny waist and he forced her to take in his entire erection. Jenna struggled, hoping to regain control, but Spencer held her in place and jerked his hips aggressively. The stabbing sensation of him burrowing deep in her pussy made Jenna cry aloud. Spencer continued raising his hips to jerk as far as he could inside her.

Maneuvering herself back into a kneeling position, Jenna resorted to grinding on Spencer as he insisted on forcing his cock further and further into her. It wasn't long before the pounding of Spencer's hard-on in combination with her clit rubbing against his pubic bone had Jenna whimpering as she orgasmed. The second her vaginal muscles clamped on Spencer's shaft, he too reached his peak and the couple climaxed in unison.

Jenna collapsed on Spencer's chest. She was tiny and petite and weighed next to nothing. With her ear over his heart, the rhythmic thumping of his heart gave her the romantic notion that it was her alone that had thawed Spencer's stony heart. As his hands stroked her hair and back, Jenna felt completely at peace. A flashback of the consecutives mornings she was forced to change Spencer's bed linen because he was entertaining a different lady every night ruined her moment. She wondered if she meant something to him or was just another woman in the long list of females he bedded.

"You're over-thinking things," he said, breaking the silence.

"How do you know?"

"Because I'm becoming very familiar with your body. You just tensed up and have become very angular and uncomfortable to have lying on top of me, whereas minutes earlier you were soft and warm and the perfect fit for me."

"Does it mean anything to you?"

"Jenna, haven't I exposed enough of myself to you for one night?" It was unlike Spencer to discuss his feelings, let alone in a restaurant. "Trust me and if you can't trust me, trust your gut feeling," he advised.

Jenna rolled off him. He wrapped an arm around her and pulled her close to him. She buried her face in his chest. Spencer's eyelids were closing and he felt himself shutting down and starting to sleep.

"You'll have to stop spoiling me like this," said Jenna.

"Mmmm. Why?"

Spencer's question was automatic and his voice lazy.

"It was Paris last weekend. A romantic getaway this weekend. You don't want me too accustomed to the good life or I'll come to expect you to whisk me away every weekend."

"I can afford that, if you'd like."

Spencer was more interested in sleep than girly chit chat.

"All the same, maybe we could stay in New York next weekend. Could be fun having a weekend together at home."

Spencer's ears pricked up and his desire to sleep was beginning to abate. He could tell from the sound of Jenna's voice she was angling for the two of them to have a weekend in New York. It was a test of sorts, but he couldn't fathom for what, exactly.

"I should think as long as we're together it wouldn't matter where we are," he said evenly.

"That's true, but as you said, I'm a family girl and New York is home. It'd be nice to have a weekend at home with the family close by."

"You see your family all week. I'd think by Saturday you'd want a break from it all. Especially as the weekend is the only time you don't have work or have babysitting duties."

"Yes, but it's New York: the city that never sleeps. I love it there. There's so much going on and so much to do. It'd be fun to explore it together as a couple, don't you think?"

"I think you should close your eyes and sleep," uttered Spencer, pretending to drift off himself.

Chapter 15

Arriving back Sunday evening, Spencer rushed to the airport to bid his family farewell as they returned to London. It wasn't until Spencer returned home in the evening that he had the time and silence to analyze a feeling of discontentment which had plagued him for the majority of the weekend.

The Jenna he'd met as his cleaner seemed to be disappearing in front of his eyes. It was as though all the qualities he'd found so attractive in her were waning. Rather than enjoying the romance and history of Portland, she spent a good part of the weekend planning the following weekend in New York. She was selecting the most exclusive clubs, best restaurants and was debating on what sized suitcase she should bring to Spencer's flat for the weekend.

When she wasn't raving about the two of them partying hard in New York, she relentlessly checked in on her cell phone and appeared to be reading constant texts, rather than interacting directly with Spencer. Spencer knew for a fact that Zada was being taken care of, Liana was staying with friends, and her mother was delighting in having a weekend free of incessant girl trouble. Although he'd advised her to keep her phone on lest her family need to get in touch, he hadn't expected her to be attached to the device all weekend.

The first night together was close to perfect, but by Saturday morning, it was like an alien had taken over Jenna's body. Nervous and twitchy, her hand was glued to her phone. She began pestering Spencer as to whether they would be leaving the Sunday night or the Monday morning.

Almost every restaurant he escorted her to she refused to eat or chose nothing more than a starter. Listless, she had no desire to explore the city. When he tried broaching the subject as to her extreme change in mood and behavior, she nearly snapped his head off, assuring him nothing was wrong and she was having a perfectly wonderful time.

At least one of us is, thought Spencer.

The lovemaking ceased after the first night. He noticed Jenna chose to wear pajamas in bed and turned her back to him. His attempt to wrap a comforting arm round her waist resulted in it being flung off and a huge divide forming between the two bodies. Her unwillingness to budge an inch and meet him halfway to discuss the personality transplant was greeted with aggression and denial.

He'd spent so much time guessing what might be bothering her, that she ended up accusing him of behaving like a bored, interfering old house wife. Spencer was at a loss as to what could be the cause. Last week in Paris, he'd treated Jenna to a new wardrobe and the best tourist attractions Paris had to offer. This weekend he'd opted for something comfortable and casual, so instead of feeling the need to impress each other, they would feel able to be themselves without pretentions. It was turning out to be a very revealing weekend.

Jenna had been warm and open and blunt in her views and opinions. He'd loved her independence and focus. Staring at her in the car driving them home from the airport, she sat with her hands folded across her chest and her head bowed low to prevent her making eye contact with him. Reluctantly Spencer acknowledged he'd made the right decision by cutting the weekend short. She was impossible.

They exchanged no words on the drive from the airport to Jenna's home. Flummoxed, Spencer still remembered his manners and thanked Jenna for spending the weekend with him. That she made no mention of meeting up and causing chaos in New York the following week, as she'd boasted when drunk, was a huge relief to the billionaire.

The driver, Graham, assisted Jenna with her luggage and saw her to her door.

"Get me home please, Graham," moaned Spencer. "I've just experienced the most disappointing dirty weekend of my life. The only thing to get dirty was my shoes when I walked along a muddy path on a

282

garden."

The sound of the chauffeur snorting loudly, cheered Graham up.

"I swear I've been conned, because the girl I took away for the weekend was not the same one that went to Paris with me."

"An evil twin perhaps," suggested Graham boldly.

"It's a possibility. I don't think I'm going to risk it a third time to find out for certain. Is it any wonder my motto is 'one night for fun, anymore then show them the door'. There were parts of the weekend that were truly excruciating. At one restaurant, I ordered a three-course meal and she chose a side salad as a main. You can imagine how scintillating the conversation was that night."

"Sir, are you vocalizing your thoughts aloud or sharing your weekend woes with me?"

"Graham, I've no intention of boring you to tears but I do need to vent. See me as a rambling mad man or a disgruntled employer – though not with your services. Perhaps I'm nothing more than a moaning rich boy. You aren't obliged to listen or offer advice, but feel free to speak your mind. I'd love your insight."

"Does she have an eating disorder?" inquired Graham.

"No. There were no rushed visits to the toilet throughout the meal."

"Mentally disturbed?"

"I didn't see any medications in her purse."

"Perhaps she forgot to pack them and that accounts for the unusual behavior."

"She wasn't crazy or having psychotic episodes. She completely retreated into herself. It shocked me. When we first met, I liked her openness and uninhibitedness when discussing an array of topics. This time she was sullen, withdrawn and did nothing but nod and agree with everything I said. It was like taking a walking doll on vacation. Her eyes glazed over. She seemed bored with me."

"Best dump her then, Mr. Lawson."

"Graham!"

"Wrong kind of advice, sir?"

"No, just unexpected."

They carried on driving in silence.

"But what if the real Jenna is lying dormant in there? Perhaps someone's repressing the girl I fell for and that's why she's been AWOL this weekend."

"Sounds a bit like something out of a science fiction novel, sir."

"It does and that makes me the hero, thus I can't dump just yet - as you so crudely put it."

"Sorry, sir," apologized Graham.

"But I am going to have to find whether the old Jenna is actually contactable or if she's disappeared for good and where and why she's gone."

Graham kept his eyes steady on the road. Part of him was amused by Spencer's boyish enthusiasm to solve the dilemma of Jenna's split personality, but another part of him wondered if Spencer was taking it a little too seriously. Spencer had a lot of connections and discovering someone's background was not difficult for him.

Having worked for Spencer for seven years, he had a degree of paternal affection for his employer. He wondered if Spencer would consider a warning to steer clear of activities that were a little excessive and underhanded if he genuinely wanted this relationship to work.

"If I may say, sir."

"I told you to speak freely, Graham."

"Rather than embroil yourself in a world of spies and

intrigue, perhaps it may be best to discuss this face-to-face with your lady friend."

"Graham, the most we talked over the weekend was when we were in the restaurants and giving our orders to the waitresses. I'm not sure the direct, normal approach is viable."

"All the same, sir. Give it a degree of consideration before planning your strategy to solve the mystery of the two-faced woman."

*

Liana and Hannah were able to extract about as much information from Jenna upon her early arrival home, as Spencer had been over the weekend. Giving each woman a kiss, Jenna murmured "good night" and removed herself to the bedroom she shared with her mother.

Her head was pounding. The headache was excruciating and no amount of aspirins would ease the pain. A cool breeze ran through the room and Jenna felt able to relax. Jenna badly wanted the vibration in her pocket to be a communication from Spencer. Habitually, she reached for the cell phone in her jeans. Not that she deserved it after her behavior that weekend, but because she wanted to hear from him, wanted the opportunity to explain.

"Nice 2 c ur home alone. Keep it that way."

She scrolled through the thread on her phone of texts from Leon. Jenna had refused to engage in communication with him and thus not responded to his many messages, but that hadn't stopped him bombarding her all weekend.

The first text arrived within minutes of her climbing in the Hummer with Spencer on Friday afternoon outside the NYU campus.

"If u go with him ull be sorry. Ur ruining things 4 us when we r meant 2 b."

She'd turned her phone off to cut Leon's method of communications with her. Unfortunately, her mother and sister were keen to get in touch and having contacted Spencer, he advised her to keep her phone on for the entire weekend, given the close-knit family may need to stay in regular contact.

Spencer initially thought the texts were sweet. What he didn't know was that the texts weren't from her mother or sister. They were all from Leon. The regularity and continuity of them eventually appeared to annoy Spencer.

"I was ur 1st and Ill be ur last. If he touches u again im going 2 have 2 make sure something happens so he wont ever want to touch u again."

That Leon had eyes on her in Portland to report to him if she'd slept with Spencer had Jenna paranoid and anxious. Concerned for Spencer's well-being, Jenna felt the only way to keep him safe was to shut down and not interact with him. She was sullen, disinterested, refused to participate in anything he suggested and answered all questions in monosyllabic remarks. She was relieved to find it was Monday tomorrow. Leon was due to start his new job. Surely, all the silliness would cease when he was actively occupying his time. Her fingers itched to dial Spencer and apologize for her appalling behavior. She'd been the guest from hell. She wouldn't even blame him if he never saw her again, that is, if he never spoke to her again. Jenna was starting to realize she'd spent all her time being critical of Spencer's abundance of wealth and shallow lifestyle choices, that she hadn't stop to consider her own decisions in life and the impact they had on her nearest and dearest.

Since when did it become acceptable to apply her unaccredited social work skills to an ex-boyfriend? It wasn't only unprofessional on her part, but if Leon hadn't meant anything to her or if she knew she hadn't been doing anything wrong, Spencer would've been the first person she'd have told about Leon's insistence in reentering her life.

The fact that she refused to confide in Spencer suggested there was a degree of loyalty to Leon that

Jenna knew was not warranted and therefore, she'd be unable to defend her feelings toward Leon if pushed on the matter.

Her best friend Kelly had warned her that no man in the early stages of dating would be thrilled to know their new partner had an ongoing relationship of sorts with an ex-partner, husband, or wife. Jenna didn't need to be told this. It was why she'd deliberately avoided discussing the situation with anyone. For the most part, Jenna considered herself to be a decent person, but regarding her actions of late, she was beginning to question it.

With no desire to enjoy the company of her mother and sister, let alone discuss her private life for some guidance, Jenna remained hiding in her bedroom. Given how spectacularly badly the weekend had gone, Jenna wasn't sure whether the kindest thing she could do was to call Spencer with an excuse of being ill and not feeling herself or deliver the news straight that she wasn't right for Spencer as she didn't match her ideals or share her vision.

Walking down the apartment block to the grassy playground, she sat on a worn swing. As she pushed the swing higher, she started to feel her head clear. When she'd discovered the photos of Spencer in a magazine, rather than rant and rave at him, she'd approached him as calmly as possible for an explanation.

She'd set precedence in their relationship by behaving like an adult over a prickly topic. There was no doubt in her mind that she owed Spencer an apology and an explanation, but that didn't necessarily mean things had to degenerate into a hateful argument.

It was early, but having been his cleaner for some time, Jenna knew Spencer's schedule.

Grimacing, she dialed his cell phone.

"Spencer Lawson, how can I help?"

"It's me – Jenna!"

"Hi Jenna," his voice was so polite and formal it frightened her.

"I was wondering if we might talk about the weekend."

"I'm not sure there's much to discuss, is there? You didn't appear to want to speak to me all on the weekend."

"I'm sure that's how it appeared, but that wasn't actually the case."

"And let me guess, you want to spend next weekend with me in New York so we can talk over everything then."

That hurt. Jenna knew her insecurities that Spencer was hiding her from the New York socialite scene was bugging her, but partying with him in public was not top on the list of her priorities.

"I don't think this talk should wait to the weekend."

"Where can I take you then?" Spencer sounded bored. Worse than that, he sounded indifferent. As if she was an obligation he had to tend to.

"I thought maybe I could take you out."

That made Spencer sit up straighter at his desk. He couldn't ever recall a woman asking to take him out. "What do you want to take me out for?"

"Because you deserve it for putting up with my outrageous behavior over the weekend. Because I'd like the opportunity to apologize and," she paused, "there's a few things happening in my life you may benefit from knowing."

"I don't know, Jenna. It's a well-intentioned proposition and please don't think I'm not appreciative of it, but you and I seem to be a lot of hard work together. I wonder if maybe we're trying to force it. I'm not sure a relationship this early on should require this enormous amount of effort."

The biting reality of his words had Jenna wanting to bawl on the spot.

"Of course. I forget your thirty-two and I'm twenty-one. You told me a while ago you weren't into girls and preferred women. I haven't behaved particularly maturely of late. Please accept my apology for the way I acted on the weekend. Portland was wonderful and so are you."

Spencer wanted to harden his heart. Jenna was only twenty-one. When he was that age, he didn't get it right every time. The difference was, when Spencer was that age he ran away from his problems. He didn't bother facing them. He locked himself in his bedroom with his computer and went to work on the many projects that would one day make him a billionaire.

"Jenna. Out of respect for you having the common decency to ring me, I'd be happy to accept your offer to take me out. I believe there are certain things in life that should be done face-to-face and not over the phone."

"Thank you, Spencer."

Seeing Spencer's ability to reassess his initial reaction to her, Jenna was keen to suggest they meet immediately. Fortunately, the filter on her brain prevented her from blurting out the words. If she wanted to demonstrate to Spencer she was mature and could be an adult, then she needed to show him she appreciated his working schedule a social life.

"When would be convenient in your schedule to meet up?"

Spencer could've cleared his schedule in a second, but feeling sorry for a young woman and wanting to pursue a relationship with her were two very different things. If he made it too soon he might be giving Jenna false hope. Leaving it a few days should communicate that the meeting was one of common courtesy, not romance.

"How are your classes on Wednesday? I could do lunch or predinner drinks before I go out if that suits."

Hearing Spencer already had plans for Wednesday night (plans she wasn't privy to) hurt her. Again, Jenna obsessed as to when the plan was made. Did he arrange them after dropping her off last night or had they been in place for some time? The thought of having drinks with Spencer and then watch him leave to meet up with another woman made Jenna physically ill.

"Wednesday lunch would be fine," stammered Jenna.

"Where should I meet you?"

"There are some decent eateries near the campus if that's not too far out of your way. We can walk from there till we find somewhere that tantalizes your taste buds."

"Are there a lot of salad bars around there?" asked Spencer drily.

Jenna actually laughed, Spencer could almost hear the golden light that was Jenna.

"I'm sure there are, but I won't lie. I'm might hungry after the weekend so I'm dying for some real meat. Honestly, I practically cleared the fridge out when I got home on Sunday."

The easiness of her voice had Spencer on the verge of falling into easy ways and asking her straight out what happened over the weekend that made her incommunicable.

"That doesn't surprise me," he said shrewdly.

"So 12 pm on Wednesday?" confirmed Jenna, keen to finish the call on a positive note.

"12 pm on Wednesday. I'll call you later so you can let me know exactly where we can meet."

*

Jenna spent the most part of Monday with a spring in her step. The phone conversation with Spencer wasn't ideal, but it hadn't been catastrophic, either. The lack of gloom and doom in his voice encouraged Jenna that it wasn't quite the time to throw in the towel in this relationship.

Jenna was back to babysitting Zada on the weeknights and though she already missed Spencer's company, both physically or over the phone, it was nice to return to a modicum of routine in her life. What thrilled her most was that there weren't any contact from Leon whatsoever. Perhaps now he had a job, he'd seen sense.

It wasn't until Tuesday morning that Jenna's world would collapse around her. Packing her bag for school, she was on the verge of leaving when Liana called and told her there was a letter addressed to her in the mail. Jenna could see straight away that the envelope was from the NYU admissions department. Confused, she dropped her bag and tore open the letter on the spot. Liana observed her sister closely as she read the letter. It was as if Jenna read through it two or three times before she was finally able to comprehend its contents.

"What's up?" asked Liana, seeing the color drain from her sister's face.

Jenna collapsed on the couch. "There's a problems with my fees."

"A problem. What do you mean?"

"I mean I've got two terms left and my most recent check was cancelled. They've represented the check and the funds weren't there."

"What's that mean?" Liana wasn't sure why she asked the question, because she knew exactly what it meant - as did Jenna.

"It means Leon told his uncle not to pay my university fees. It means I have to self-fund or pull out."

"You can't pull out with only two terms to go," said Liana, incredulously.

"But we don't have the money to fund my fees, either. There's no way our household earns enough to be considered by a bank for a loan to cover the costs and even if we were, I'd be spending more time working to meet the monthly payments than actually studying."

Liana swore strongly. Jenna couldn't be bothered to chastise her sister by reminding her of baby Zada's presence.

"This is Leon, isn't it?" inquired Liana.

"Yes, it is."

"What are your options?"

"I need to go to the university first and see what they suggest and then formulate a plan from there."

"Jen, I'm so sorry. I can't believe he'd do this to

you."

"Neither can I," concurred a wounded Jenna.

The news from the admissions office wasn't positive. Jenna didn't qualify for scholarships, nor financial help under extraordinary circumstances. She was able to put her studies on hold until she had the money to pay for her final two terms, but that was the only real option available. She sat on the campus grounds for hours, tears streaming down her cheeks, wondering what on earth she was going to do.

"You'll do what your mother did," she told herself, "you'll get a job, work hard and make ends meet. Maybe you'll have enough money to save up and get your degree one day, maybe you won't, but you'll conduct yourself as a decent, hardworking human being."

It should've sounded like a pep talk to buzz her up, but the silent tears became sobs as she saw her dreams slipping away from her. She studied hard for this degree. She didn't have Liana's natural brains so she'd invested a lot of time and effort obtaining her admirable grades. She dreamed of helping kids like herself out of the circumstances they were born into, so they could have a dream and achieve it. The truth was, she was just another kid from the block that had the big dream she couldn't make come true. She was a joke. She'd disappointed everyone.

Telling her mother the news would be the most heartbreaking. Jenna's mother was infinitely proud of her daughter's commitment to her studies and to have to walk away because of a lousy ex-boyfriend would break her heart.

Their lousy father walked out on them leaving Hannah a single mom. She'd done her best to raise independent daughters, but Jenna threw away her teenage years skipping school and getting up to all sorts of foolish things. Jenna fell in love with a charismatic, handsome, silver-tongued boy who t was more comfortable with a gun in his hand than a calculator or pen. Jenna was merely repeating the cycle her mother strove so hard to break.

There was no point in attending classes. Jenna headed home. Keen to avoid Liana, she spent the afternoon in the playground. Few children used the area, so Jenna didn't feel or look out of place as she made use of the equipment.

"Remember when we used to play on here late at night?"

Jenna raised her head to see Leon. Wordlessly she jumped off the roundabout.

"Where you going, girl?"

She opened the gate and walked past him.

"Jenna, why you gotta be like this? Why are you fighting what's natural?"

An anger Jenna had never known bubbled inside her. She wanted to slap his face, pound her fists on his chest, and scream at him.

"That's what a girl would do," she reminded herself. "A woman would keep her dignity intact and leave without making a scene."

"You know I can make this right for us, babe? All you gotta do is give me one date. One date and I swear I'll pay those fees up front for both terms the next day. One date and if it doesn't work out, I'll leave you alone. I'll still pay the fees, but I won't harass you. I promise you. I'm a man of my word."

Jenna remembered Leon's promise that when he was released from jail he would keep his distance from her so she could get on with her life. He'd not only broken that promise, but gone out of his way to destroy the future she'd been working so hard to provide for herself. It was on the tip of her tongue to remind him of that broken promise.

"He's not worth the effort," she reminded herself, before walking back to her apartment block.

Hannah was surprised to see her daughter lying listless on the couch when she came in from work past 11 pm.

"Where's that handsome billionaire of yours?"

"He's not mine, Mom."

"You didn't say much about the weekend. Not as compatible as you thought?"

"Mom, he's a billionaire and I'm...well look at us – look at what we are."

"He didn't strike me as a man driven solely by money. I thought he was making a real effort in terms of our family."

"He was."

"Then what?"

"Mom, how would you define an independent woman?"

Hannah lifted her daughter's feet and sat on the sofa. She was quiet for a while contemplating the answer. "I believe an independent woman is a woman who isn't subject to another person's authority. She's free from control and free to make her own choices in life."

"And she never relies on a man for money?"

"She never relies on a man for money, no," agreed

Hannah, "but she knows when to ask for a helping hand to achieve what she wants. She also knows the right helping hand to choose. Asking for help isn't a sign of weakness or ineptitude, it actually demonstrates a woman with a realistic vision on how life works.

But never, ever ask for a helping hand if it means you losing your freedom, because then you become reliant on others and I don't think that's a good thing for any man or woman." Her mother was silent for a minute, then asked, "Have you asked the billionaire for money?"

"No," snapped Jenna indignantly.

"I imagine someone of his caliber would hate being used for money. You need to tread carefully there. He's the type of man that will wine and dine you, but you need to show him your appreciation and I'm not talking about in the bedroom. Treat him with respect. Trust him. Involve him with your dreams. Otherwise he'll feel used."

"I have a feeling I got this whole feisty independent woman act completely muddled up and I think Spencer's a casualty in my ignorance."

"Spencer's a big boy. I'm sure he can handle the mistakes of a twenty-one year old if he wants to."

"And if he doesn't want to."

"Then he's not the man for you. He's handsome, polite, well spoken, his brown eyes are so caring, he's effortlessly charming, and I can see how much you'd like him to be your knight in shining white armor. I'd love for him to rescue you from this apartment and give you the kind of surroundings where all your dreams come true, but sometimes life isn't a fairytale. Sometimes we have to accept that just because we love with all our heart it doesn't mean they'll love us back with the same ferocity."

"It doesn't seem fair."

"No. I loved your father. I loved him to the moon and back, but he never loved me the same way. Deep down I probably always knew that, but I kept hoping things would change. If we got married, he might love me more, if we had a baby he'd see me differently, if we had a family he'd want to be a part of it.

He should never have led me on to believe those things, but if I'd taken care right when we started dating, I'd have noticed things that highlighted the differences in our feelings for one another. Perhaps I'd have made different choices. I wouldn't be without you or Liana, but I wonder if I'd gone in with open eyes how our lives might've been different."

"What's the moral of that horrid fairytale?"

"The moral of the story is - don't believe in the dream. Create it but don't pretend it already exists."

"I wanted to love him."

"But now you've spent more time with Spencer, you realize you don't?"

"No. Now I've spent more time with Spencer I realize I do. It's just that I was playing at being a princess, pretending to be someone I'm not. I don't know how he feels about me and he can't possibly say how he feels about me because I've flitted between being Jenna and some independent princess that doesn't need a man. I got frightened by how fairylike our tale started that I stopped acting naturally and tried acting in a way I thought he expected. He may never give me a second chance."

Jenna waited for her mother to assure her that Spencer would certainly give her a second chance.

"Jenna, you can only be honest with him and be yourself. The choice is his, not yours."

"I thought I was doing the right thing."

"I'm sure he'll take that into account. A man like him lives in a complicated world, maybe the reason he liked you was because you've always been simple, direct and straight to the point. No pretensions."

"So there is still hope?"

"Jenna, no relationship can survive if there's no trust. I can't predict the outcome of your predicament. I'm a cleaner, not a fortune teller. It sounds clichéd, baby girl, but love hurts. I'm only your mother. I'll cheer you on when you need it and pick up the pieces if you shatter and I'll cross my fingers and hope you find true happiness with the right person."

There was no point crying and no point telling her mom about the university fees dilemma. It could all wait until the morning, because whatever happened, Jenna knew her mother was right by her side and not going to abandon her under any circumstances and no matter how many silly mistakes she was prone to making in her youth.

Chapter 16

Spencer was surprised by Jenna's suggestion that they meet at the Washington Square Arch. True, it was only a stone's throw from her university's campus, but given they were meeting for lunch, he wasn't sure where she was intending on taking him. Dressed in his usual suit for work, he smiled inwardly as Jenna came into his vision. She was dressed in jeans and an NYU slim fitting pastel pink t-shirt. It made him remember how young she was. She was lugging a wicker hamper.

"I wasn't sure we'd be able to agree on a place to eat and I knew you'd be limited for time, so I thought I'd bring lunch."

Habitually, as he did with all female friends, Spencer gave her a quick kiss on the cheek. He took the hamper.

"Any ideas on where the best place to sit is?" he enquired.

As it was the last of the summer season, the park was throbbing with people.

"There's a fountain nearby. It's crowded, but I find it sweet to watch the kids and carefree tourists playing in the water."

Spencer followed her lead. Having found a suitable spot, Jenna laid out a blanket and opened the basket.

"I hope the wine's stayed chilled. You get these gadgets that claim to keep them chilled, but you never know how effective they are. For all I know, it may have ended up making the sandwiches soggy."

"She's nervous," thought Spencer.

He was filled with pity. She'd clearly gone to a huge degree of effort to pack the hamper and wanted everything to be perfect. He placed his hand over Jenna's and felt it shaking.

"Jenna, it's okay. I'm not in a rush and I doubt anything's spoiled. Let's take our time and unpack so we can relax."

Jenna wanted to cry at how perfectly sensitive he was. They unpacked miniature scotch eggs, pork pies and Cornish pasties. There were cucumber, egg and lettuce, and smoked salmon and cream cheese sandwiches, as well as cold chicken and quiches. For something sweeter, she'd included scones, Battenberg cake and strawberries and fresh cream. Jenna had a red and white wine, a rose and a flask of earl grey and breakfast tea.

"I don't know what half this stuff is, but on the internet it said this was a British picnic hamper. Some of the bits, I could make at home, but other things I had to buy."

Spencer was touched by her endeavors. The whole date was reinforcing in him their age gap and the error of judgment he'd made by contemplating a relationship with Jenna. It had nothing to do with money; she didn't have the life experience for them to be a successful couple.

"Jenna, I can't tell you how impressed I am by the effort. I can't think of any girl that's ever gone to this much trouble for me."

Jenna's smile was heartbreaking. Spencer girded his loins. Ending any relationship whether amicable or not was never pleasant.

They ate in silence and watched the children splash in the fountains and the tourists' debate on whether they should paddle or not.

"If I didn't have work to go back to, I'd be half inclined to join them," said Spencer finally breaking the silence.

"Me too," agreed Jenna.

It was the opening she needed to initiate conversation.

"Spencer about the weekend."

Spencer wasn't sure whether to make eye contact with her or not. He flicked his eyes towards her to acknowledge he was listening, but reverted back to the wet and wild scene in front of him lest he intimidate her clearly rehearsed speech.

"I haven't been totally honest with you. The night we got back from Paris, it transpired that Leon, my ex-boyfriend, had been released from jail."

Jenna could see Spencer's body stiffen.

"I knew you already knew of his existence from the private investigator, and disapproved. I thought it prudent not to tell you."

She saw Spencer hurl the remnants of his quiche towards a pigeon for it to finish.

"Leon and I made a promise to one another that when he was released we'd steer clear of one another, because together we'd been nothing but trouble. Apart, we both seemed to have made progress in our lives. With that in mind, I really didn't think it worth mentioning. Only...."

"Only Leon didn't steer clear of you and you didn't keep your distance from him," said Spencer frostily.

"How did you know? You had a private investigator on me again?"

"No," said Spencer slowly. "It makes sense. It's not even a lucky guess. A simple and correct deduction."

"Leon was making a real effort when he came out. He got a job and he was behaving like a changed man. I think that jail sentence forced him to reconsider his life and make positive changes. The trouble was, he thought that because we'd both matured and changed that maybe our relationship had, too."

Spencer sat as still as a statue.

"I didn't feel the same way. At first I felt sorry for him. I figured he was lonely. His old friends were still part of the gang he once ran with so he couldn't hang out with them. He had no new friends. It was natural that he'd gravitate toward me as the only person he knew. I want to be a social worker. I thought if I didn't respond to his overtures for friendship or companionship, it may send him back down a dangerous path.

I didn't want to see that happen. Not after all the effort he made. For me, it was nothing more than a professional desire to help. Maybe I felt some obligation because of our history, but nothing more than that. But Leon wanted more. When I said no, it felt like he was threatening me."

"Did you go to the police?"

"No. I hoped it would go away. He's started a new job. I figured he'd make new friends and get a new girlfriend. But he seems determined that we should try again. When you met me last Friday to go to Portland, he sent a text. I don't know if he had a friend watching me or if he was following me, but it freaked me out. That's why I turned my phone off."

"And I told you to turn it back on again."

"Yeah. But Mom and Liana only wanted to touch base; the excessive texts were from Leon. It may sound over the top, but I was worried about your safety. I thought if I kept my distance then maybe I could protect you. I drove a huge wedge between us, which has separated us, so I guess I did protect you, but I don't want to be apart from you. I only wanted to make sure Leon wouldn't hurt you."

"The road to hell is paved with good intentions – isn't that what they say?"

"Can't we pave a road back to some place nice?" suggested Jenna.

Spencer was silent. In a way, he was glad he'd met Jenna. The conversation had cleared certain matters up. Jenna wasn't using him for money and he obviously wasn't as dull as clay in respect of being boyfriend material. The confession didn't change anything. It didn't make him want to be with Jenna. It just made him feel sorry for her.

"I don't think so, Jenna. I'm glad to hear you've seen the light with this Leon, because however legitimate he may be since finishing his term in jail, I don't think he's the kind of guy who is going to be able to support your dreams in life. You need to wise up. Not every man that's kind to you or speaks nicely to you is going to be Mr. Right. You can't rescue everyone, especially if it's at the cost of your own...."

"Happiness?" said Jenna, filling in the blank for Spencer.

"Were you happy with me?" asked Spencer.

"Intimidated, out of place, immature, patronized, lacking in manners – I was all those things around you, but I can promise you, I was never unhappy with you Spencer. I was genuinely happy with you when it was only us two."

"And by reaching out to Leon you threw away your chance of happiness."

Jenna's heart beat faster and she felt she might be sick. This wasn't how she wanted things to go. This wasn't what she wanted to hear.

"What a waste," said Spencer glumly.

He packed the hamper up for Jenna, signaling the

conversation had ended. In his haste to pack, Jenna thought he might roll her clean off the blanket and onto the grass.

"Can I ask you a question Spencer?"

"There's no point now, Jenna. I really respect you explaining to me about Portland. It actually has put my mind at rest about a lot of questions and self doubts I had. And I'm sure you're stunned by the fact that a billionaire could possibly have insecurities. Before you, I was content being a playboy. I tried dating with you and it went so horrendously wrong it got me thinking that maybe by nature I'm not designed to have one partner.

This conversation has made me realize that I am ready to settle down and I'm not a bad guy. I do have potential as a boyfriend, maybe even as a husband. Thank you for giving me that. If we hadn't talked I'd have taken the blame for everything and maybe never tried finding love again. Now I'm free to and it's an exciting prospect."

"If I've given you all that, surely you can permit me to ask one question," insisted Jenna, taking the hamper from Spencer's hand.

"Go ahead."

"If I'd been honest with you, from the very

beginning, from the second I found out Leon was released from jail, would it have changed anything?"

"It would've changed everything."

Jenna shut her eyes so she didn't have to memorize the picture of Spencer Lawson walking away from her.

The Final Chapter

Spencer didn't feel good about the way he'd left things with Jenna. It would be a lot easier if he could attribute his impulsive cold behavior at the end down to rage and anger, but that wasn't the case. He was hurt and he was envious. Hurt that Jenna hadn't trusted him. Envious that he'd finished things that left Leon in a position to win Jenna back. Leon would be waiting for her, sympathetic, understanding why her head had been turned by a billionaire and ultimately he'd be Jenna's final choice.

Leon would be Jenna's choice because Spencer hadn't been prepared to give Jenna any other options. He hadn't had the courage to accept that people are flawed and make mistakes. He felt she'd made a fool of him and he couldn't let it happen a second time. In truth, there probably would never have been a second time. She'd have learned from that relationship mistake.

He'd been so self-righteous about Jenna's actions, he hadn't stopped to think that she may have had good reason to make particular choices regarding discussing Leon with him. After all, hadn't Spencer been the one to have a private investigator explore Jenna's past? Hadn't he been overly vocal about his disapproval of her connection with Leon? Hadn't he hidden her from the public eye and refused to be seen with her publicly to protect her from the paparazzi? Was that his decision to make or was it something he should've discussed with her?

She may not have become obsessed with a weekend in New York if he'd trusted her enough to explain that he had concerns that the attention he attracted in the tabloids regarding his social life might put her off wanting to date him. Jenna had omitted to tell him about Leon because she felt it made her a less attractive dating prospect. With time to reflect, Spencer could completely understand her reasoning, even if he didn't fully agree with it.

He was therefore happy to find a couple of weeks after their picnic, he had an appointment scheduled in his diary by his personal assistant for a fifteen minute meeting with a Ms. Jenna King. There was no further information on what the meeting entailed, but Spencer was pleased Jenna had been able to convince his PA to allocate her a little spot in his busy diary.

To the outside world, Spencer remained calm and unmoved by the sudden disappearance of Jenna from his life. He acted as though she was no different to any of the other women that passed through his social diary. She was only the lucky one that lasted somewhat longer than the others.

Almost unwilling to admit it to himself, Spencer was

hoping that Jenna's wish to see him was to discuss how they'd left things after the picnic and whether there was room for negotiation so that they may pursue their relationship again. Another part of him was dreading seeing her in case she was there to gloat about reconnecting with Leon and reveling in an engagement to the ex-con or some such thing. He couldn't imagine Jenna being that petty or small minded, but hell hath no fury like a woman scorned. Spencer's icy behavior toward her when she opened her heart to him in Washington Square did not make him come across as a particularly nice person. She was well within her rights to hold a grudge.

He was pacing the office in the half hour leading up to her arrival. When his personal assistant announced Jenna King had arrived, he took a deep breath and advised his PA to send her in. Jenna was dressed formally in a business suit. Spencer was unsure how to greet her. He'd never seen her in business attire. It was a simple navy skirt suit with matching blazer and respectable stockings and heels. She appeared older than her years and very confident and composed.

"Mr. Lawson," she said offering a hand, "or would you be more comfortable with me calling you Spencer."

There was nothing unfriendly in her tone, but Spencer had an urge to remind her that he'd made love to her and held her while she slept. He pushed the sentimental feelings aside.

"Given our history, Spencer is fine," he replied. "Am I to call you Ms. King or is the informal Jenna acceptable."

"Jenna's fine," she smiled.

The smile lit up her face and Spencer suddenly realized what a complete pig-headed fool he'd been with Jenna. She was twenty-one and juggling the responsibilities of someone much older than her years – of course she was going to drop the ball on occasion. How could he have been so unforgiving?

"Take a seat."

Jenna sat demurely in the antique wooden chair. It looked impressive, but was distinctly uncomfortable. Spencer observed her wringing her hands. She was as nervous as he was.

"What can I do for you?"

"It's to do with helping me out of a bind. One you predicted as it happens. My tendency is to see the best in people."

"That's not a bad quality, Jenna," interjected Spencer.

"Perhaps not, but it's not necessarily how the world

works. If I run around permanently with rose-colored glasses on, I probably won't advance too far. Trusting someone's best qualities meant that I refused to acknowledge their not so good qualities. That lack of objectivity has ultimately left me in a very difficult situation."

Spencer clasped his hands together and stared intently at Jenna waiting for her to continue.

"You warned me as soon as you discovered Leon's background that his paying my university tuition may come at a price. You said however good his intentions were at the time, he'd have something to dangle over my head if he needed to."

"Are you in trouble with the police?" asked Spencer sternly.

"No, of course not. However, he's refusing to make the final two payments of my university course. The final payment for this term is due this Friday. If I can't get the money together I'll have to pull out until I'm in a position whereby I can afford the fees."

"Why is Leon withholding the money?"

"Because I'm refusing to go on a date with him."

"So if you go on a date with him he'll pay the final fees for the course?"

"That's correct."

"But you won't play ball?"

"No. I'm not going to prostitute myself out for anyone. The incentive to join you at the charity gala dinner wasn't the $1000 check, it was the fact that you wanted my company. I was your first choice when your original date pulled out.

No matter how important the university fees are, I can't compromise my own morals and date someone who I know isn't right for me. Why would I want to even give my relationship with Leon a second chance when he's stooped to such low tactics? I won't lie, he has turned his life around, but there are certain characteristics to him that I don't like. It would never work out," explained Jenna.

"And you remembered I said I'd be your patron and cover the cost of your fees because I think the skills you're obtaining from this social work degree are worth endorsing," said Spencer smoothly.

"I did remember that, but I'm here for a helping hand not a handout. Don't worry, I'm not asking you to create a Jenna King College charity, you've enough on your plate with your other philanthropic works."

Spencer maintained a straight face, determined not to give any emotion away.

"As I rightly highlighted, if I did accept your patronage I'd be putting myself into a position where I'd end up owing you a favor to be called upon at any time."

"Except I'm not Leon and I wouldn't do that to you," he said quietly.

"I know. That's why I decided to bring my proposition to you."

"What proposition is that?"

"Spencer, it's a huge thing to ask and if I thought for a second it would put any financial strain on you, I wouldn't have made this appointment. You did, however, offer once and I need to take you up on it. I was wondering if you could loan me the money to cover my fees. It'd be such a waste to pull out of the course when I've nearly completed it. There's no guarantee I'd get a loan from a financial institution and the repayments would mean me taking on extra work that would inevitably eat into my study time.

If I borrowed the money from you, I could pay it back once I've finished the course. I already have a placement for the summer that should lead to a full time job enabling me to make the payments, with interest included, pretty quickly after I've graduated."

"You could just let me pay the fees. I could have a

legal document drawn up saying that you are under no legal obligation to repay them to put your conscience at rest."

"That's very generous of you Spencer, but I can't accept that. Is there any way you'll consider my proposition?" reiterated Jenna.

"Yes, of course," said Spencer vehemently. "There was never any question of that. Consider it done. I want you to finish the course and I'm really pleased you came to me and asked for help. It can't have been easy, given how we left things. Your qualifications are paramount. I only wanted you to reconsider the terms."

"That's kind, but doing it this way we're equals."

"We are," affirmed Spencer, "but it's an interest-free loan – that is my one condition."

"Fine," agreed Jenna with a mock sigh. "I guess my time is up."

Spencer had an urge to invite Jenna out for lunch, but he knew she wouldn't accept. She'd grown up. With time and perspective she'd have been able to see how immaturely he'd behaved and that didn't make him anymore an attractive dating prospect to Jenna, than Leon was.

They shook hands.

Spencer watched her leave. He felt a slight turn of nausea knowing instinctually there would only ever be one Jenna King in his life.

*

Four weeks had passed since Jenna's visit and the only contact Spencer had with her was authorizing a wire transfer to her bank account with the relevant monies she needed to pay the university fees. She'd sent him a thank you card and left him the details of her summer placement and assured him she'd keep in touch regarding her employment status. It was all polite and perfect. Spencer always knew they'd come from different worlds but never had the differences in their lives been so confronting.

He'd become accustomed to spending nights in at his flat and his social life was almost non-existent, but despite his general heartache it transpired that the world continued to turn. Spencer was due to attend an event. It wasn't his own charity, but it was an event run by the publicist he employed for his own charity works, thus he felt obliged to go. There was no need for a date or even a requirement to be there for a particularly long period, but manners dictated he make an appearance. After all, she was responsible for gathering guests to his functions so it was only right he return the favor.

There was a time Spencer saw Saturday nights as the

pinnacle of the week, but there was little enthusiasm he could muster for facing the women that would flock to him and the paparazzi waiting to see who he'd escort home.

He dressed in his usual snappy attire of a three-piece suit. As soon as he entered the large club, he was greeted by his publicist with a kiss on the cheek and found himself being ushered toward many single and suitable women for him to take his pick of. Spencer couldn't deny the women were gorgeous and glamorous, but his loins seemed unexcited when he engaged with them in light conversation. They seemed to spend their time gushing over him or sticking to shallow surface talk.

For the first time ever, Spencer decided to skulk away into the shadows. He stood on the outskirts of the room observing how everyone behaved and interacted. It might be for a good cause, but as he saw men and women eyeing one another up, he thought the whole scene irreverent. He'd graduated from that phase of his life. He no longer wanted his personal life to be something splashed on the pages of a tabloid. Shaking his head, he checked his watch to see how long he'd have to wait before he could leave without too guilty a conscience. As he looked up, his eyes made contact with those of a waitress standing with a tray of canapés standing directly opposite him on the other side of the room.

It was Jenna.

Curiosity piqued, Spencer was unable to help himself and made his way over to her with quick strides. A sense of relief washed over him when he saw Jenna wait his approach, rather than choose to scuttle away under the guise of work.

"What are you doing here?"

"Spencer, I'm dressed as a waitress serving balsamic glazed pecans with rosemary and sea salt, I would have thought the answer to that question was very obvious?"

"Let me rephrase that. How come you aren't working for Supreme Cleaning Services?"

"I am. I've taken on part time work for the weekends that's all," she said stiffly, maintaining a smile on her face. "Sorry about the stilted answers," she apologized, "I am on duty. Can't afford to be seen slacking."

"Why do you need to take on extra work? I thought the whole purpose of paying your university fees via a loan was so that you wouldn't have to take on extra jobs and could focus on your studies."

"It was. My situation has changed somewhat. I need to save a little extra money."

"Anything in particular?"

"Yes, but now isn't the time or place to discuss it."

"Then when?" asked Spencer boldly.

"What makes you think you have a right as to involve yourself in my plans?"

"I don't suppose I do, really. It's just that," Spencer paused and deliberately looked away from Jenna, "I still care about you."

"That's nice to hear."

Spencer turned and smiled at her. He could see her smile was genuine. Her expression read as a mixture of relief and hope.

"When do you get a break?" pressed Spencer.

"Not for at least another hour."

"Can I accompany you?"

"Spencer, it'll be for fifteen minutes out by the fire escape. It's pretty chilly tonight."

"I don't mind."

"You're bored out of your brain. I've been watching you and you aren't even attempting to strike up a conversation with anyone."

"So you had your eye on me?" he asked cheekily.

"Every woman has," chuckled Jenna. "I saw every female's head spin when you entered and checked to see who was causing the big stir. When I saw it was you...well it was entertaining to see how you operate in these situations. I always had you pegged as more of a flirt and an extrovert."

"People change," said Spencer softly.

"They certainly do."

They stood in silence.

"Spencer?"

"Yes."

"You can't stand by my side the entire night tonight. I'm going to have to circulate."

"Is that your way of giving me the brush off?"

"No, that's my way of saying I can't afford to lose this job. I'll give you a signal when I'm due on my break."

Without thinking, Spencer kissed her cheek and made his way to the bar. Jenna's hand flew to her face. The electricity when he touched her was still super charged. It was as if the imprint of his lips had burnt a mark on her face. She could feel her eyes welling and began to stomp around the room to offer the food to the guests. Keeping herself busy, the next ninety minutes flew by. A fellow waiter tapped her on the shoulder to notify her of her break.

Passing the bar, she gave Spencer a wave. Leaving his drink, he followed her out.

"It is chilly out here," he noted as Jenna insisted on heaving open the fire exit. "Is it inappropriate of me to offer you my jacket?"

"Not at all," shivered Jenna, "but you very may well regret it."

Spencer slung it over her shoulders and shivered himself.

"You look radiant tonight Jenna."

"In this outfit?" she laughed.

"I don't know. The traditional waitress uniform has its benefits. Shows off your legs and cleavage; no man will criticize that. It's a huge improvement on the Supreme Cleaning Service polo shirt and jeans."

Jenna laughed. "There was a compliment somewhere in there, so thank you."

"I know it's not my place to say it, but I'm proud of you, Jenna."

"Why?"

"Because you changed. You grew up in front of my eyes. You've lost none of the qualities that I fell for, but you've gained so much more in how you approach life. At first, you were a girl trying to deal with a woman's problem, now I see a strong woman directing and controlling everything life throws her way. It's an amazing change to witness."

"That almost hints at you having fallen in love with me."

"Almost," smirked Spencer into the dark night.

The lack of moonlight made the darkness heavy, almost suffocating.

"For what it's worth, I don't think I would've changed without you stepping in my life," admitted Jenna.

"My only regret is that I stepped out of it so quickly," confessed Spencer.

Without another word, the couple kissed.

*

Spencer was going to be the last to leave the party. His acquaintances seemed relieved to see the old Spencer back on the scene. The female singletons were vying for his attention throughout the duration of the evening, rejecting other advances from eligible bachelors on a thin thread of hope that Spencer may choose them. But Spencer chose none of them.

He waited patiently as the waiting staff cleared up. Even then, some women chose to loiter, wondering if they would have a final opportunity to outsmart the competition. Jenna appeared in her waitress uniform with a thin cardigan.

"Are we leaving through the back entrance?"

"No," said Spencer firmly. "We're going via the front, unless you're uncomfortable with that."

As they stepped out, Spencer holding Jenna's hand tightly, the flash of cameras blinded them both. Spencer held up a hand to dull his vision to see his town car, but made no attempt to cover Jenna up or disguise with whom he was leaving the premises.

Graham leaped out of the driver's seat and opened the door for the couple to get in the limo. Taking his place, they drove slowly away from the mounting paparazzi.

"And where are we headed, sir?" asked Graham politely.

"That would be Jenna's choice."

"Back to yours," asserted Jenna. "We have some talking to do."

Arriving at Spencer's apartment building, Jenna smiled as she was reminded of her many visits here as a cleaner.

"Nothing changes, hey?" said Spencer.

"Everything changes," she contradicted him.

As they took the lift up and Spencer opened the door to the penthouse suite the two of them were transported to the very first night Jenna accompanied Spencer as his date to the charity gala dinner.

Spencer led her to the bedroom and sat on the bed, his legs spread wide.

"We need to talk," Jenna said kindly.

"We have all the time in the world to talk, Jenna, but right now that waitress outfit is really doing it for me," he uttered. "Take it off – slowly."

Jenna shook her head. Spencer sensed it wasn't out of rejection; he could only attribute her reluctance to being body shy.

Standing up, Spencer walked toward her. Closing his eyes, he bowed his head to meet her lips. The kiss was warm and soft and Jenna felt herself caught up in the emotion the two had never managed to say to one another.

He pulled at white strap of her apron and let it slide to the ground. Fingers tentatively exploring her garment, he found a button at the back of her neck. Unbuttoning it and lowering the zip. he loosened the black waitress uniform. From there, he tugged it over her arms and watched the material gather toward her waist.

Her black bra was tantalizing against her dark skin. Spencer reached behind and unclasped the clip. Her pert breasts fell and he shut his eyes again as his hands went to cup them. The hardening of her nipples at his touch and exposure to the cool air of the flat had his cock hardening.

Spencer kissed her more deeply, letting his tongue press into her mouth. As he did so, he let one hand wriggle between her thighs and move its way upward. His hand cupped the crotch of her panties and could feel dampness through the cotton. He moaned in her mouth.

Jenna ground against his cupped hand, enjoying the feel of the mound of Spencer's palm on her clit. Removing his hand from between her legs, Spencer returned to her waitress uniform and finished unzipping it. He was able to push it over her slender hips.

Jenna, topless in her underwear, stockings and heels was a picture he'd never forget.

"Climb on the bed on all fours," he ordered.

Jenna shook her head.

"Not like that," she murmured.

Spencer nodded. He slipped out of his own jacket and unbuttoned his shirt at lightning speed. Gracefully, he undid his trousers and kicked them and his shoes and socks aside. Spencer was left standing in his tight-legged Calvin Klein boxers. Jenna couldn't resist letting her hands trace the outline of his upper body and masculine arms. Spencer permitted Jenna to caress him awhile before continuing with proceedings.

He dropped to his knees and undid her suspender belt. Taking his time, he rolled her stockings down, letting his hands appreciate the shape of her legs. He assisted Jenna out of her shoes. Just as gently, he rolled her panties down. Lacing his fingers through hers, he drew her toward the bed. Throwing the sheets back, he climbed in and patted the spot next to him. Jenna's hazel eyes looked into Spencer's deeply as if to decide whether this was a fatal mistake or a beautiful beginning. Convinced of her decision, she crept in and curled up next to Spencer.

As he spooned her, she could feel his erection pressed firmly against her buttocks. Reaching behind, she attempted to work her hands into his underwear and grip his heavenly cock. Spencer shoved his own boxers down and relished the firm grip of Jenna's hand on his throbbing hard-on. Lifting Jenna's leg, she immediately released his rod from her grasp. Spencer held the base of his prick and rubbed the shaft between her plump dripping pussy lips. He could feel Jenna's slight frame quivering next to his solid bulk.

Slowly, he eased the helmet of his cock into her tight slit. She gasped and relaxed when she realized Spencer was in no hurry. He inched himself in slowly and glided gently in and out of her. Due to his length, the bulb of his cock was rubbing against the wall of her vagina. To shallow the penetration, Spencer dislodged himself completely.

Twisting Jenna until she was laying flat on her back, he climbed between her legs and once again penetrated her in a traditional missionary style. The sex wasn't fast and fanatic, but it didn't need to be. The length and girth of Spencer was satisfying for Jenna and the tightness of Jenna's slit was an ecstasy Spencer had never known.

As Jenna wrapped her legs around Spencer's waist, he knew he was able to gradually increase the pace of their lovemaking. Jenna groaned as his cock stretched her, but the weight of Spencer on her and his hot breath on her face had her hips grinding and seeking her own climax. As Spencer thrust hard and deep to orgasm, Jenna peaked seconds afterwards clawing her fingers into Spencer's bottom to drive him in further and then wrapped her arms round his shoulders so she could enjoy his body settled on hers.

They were melded as one by sweat and sex and silence. Eventually, Spencer rolled off and took Jenna in his arms to sleep.

"We still need to talk," she said.

"I told you we have all the time in the world to talk."

"Actually we've got less than nine months."

Spencer's eye lids fluttered opened. He suddenly found himself with renewed energy.

"Are you saying what I think you're saying?"

"I'm saying I'm pregnant with your child," said Jenna calmly. "I was going to wait till the three month mark before I told you just to be certain, but as fate brought us together tonight..."

"Why didn't you say something earlier?"

"Because it wasn't the right time for either of us. I

wanted the baby because I love you and that was the reason for me to keep it. I knew you'd want the baby with or without me. I didn't want you feeling obligated to be a part of the child's life."

"But I want to be," said Spencer, indignantly.

"Like you want to be a part of my life?"

"Of course."

"Why do you want to be a part of my life Spencer?"

"Because," he paused. "because I love you."

"I know you do," she said smugly. "You once told me you'd wait as long it takes for me when you had no idea what was going on in my life. Anyone who says that must have love in their heart for the person. I had a lot of growing up to do. I think I'm in a position now to accept your love and I know I'm a person that's able to love you properly."

Spencer kissed her.

"You won't throw away that waitress outfit just yet will you? I kind of like the idea of the paparazzi photographing you in it tomorrow when we leave to visit your family. It'll be like we've come full circle again. The billionaire and the hired help."

Jenna groaned. "I'll be sure to wear it out so the

tabloids get a final story on your love life, but then it's going in the trash."

"I don't know. You might want to keep it for special occasions," teased Spencer.

Jenna slapped him. He caught her hands to stop her play fighting. Gently, he put his hand on her belly. "I think we've got the perfect story to tell this one when he or she is old enough," said Spencer seriously.

"So do I."

THE END

*Did you enjoy this story please **leave a rating** on the store.*

Remember, by leaving a good review you are helping to support this independent author and the indie author industry in general!

BILLIONAIRE IMPOSSIBLE

Amalia Parker is a hard working woman who is determined to reach the top in her career. She has no time for love however when certain men walk into your life you simply have to find the time.

Matthew Sellars is a self-made billionaire who is incredibly handsome with a charming personality also. He is in the top 1% of men who have it all. Most women would consider a man like him impossible to get.

When Matthew and Malia meet there is an undeniable attraction. They both know they should not get involved with each other but they can not help themselves and for a while it is good. Very good.

However, Matthew has a dark secret. A secret so dark it promises to ruin everything before it even started.

Is this relationship going to end up being an

IMPOSSIBLE mission for the cute couple?
Or can true love make anything possible?

CPSIA information can be obtained at www.ICGtesting.com
Printed in the USA
LVOW04s1432290915

456191LV00017B/533/P